IN PLAIN SIGHT

A Novel

Richard DeVeau

Library and Archives Canada Cataloguing in Publication
DeVeau, Richard, author
In Plain Sight/Richard DeVeau

Issued in print and electronic formats.

ISBN: 978-1-998501-77-9 (paperback)
ISBN: 978-1-998501-78-6 (ebook)

Cover Design: Axel Peralta
Interior Design: James M. Leslie

Warpath Press
Toronto, Ontario, Canada
www.warpathpress.com

To Elizabeth, Christopher, Michelle, Anna, Lucas, and Lillian—six beats of my heart.

"The state within a state is hiding mostly in plain sight."
— Mike Lofgren

Chapter 1

The gunshots made her jump. Even though Eve Tuant was ready, she flinched two more times as the nearby line of seven Green Berets fired the remaining volleys of their twenty-one-gun salute into the cloudless, cerulean, June-afternoon sky.

The veterans' section of the Birchview Cemetery was nearly as packed as the church had been. Everywhere a sea of blue police uniforms, a few black suits and dresses peppered in. A vast green plot of row after row of identical white crosses was bordered on three sides by thick woods of birch, oak, scrub pine and maple. People were even standing among the trees a few rows deep.

A warm, briny breeze blew across Eve's face. The source of it could be heard at the bottom of the steep hill three hundred yards away, where a steady beat of ocean waves took turns slapping the large granite boulders of Gloucester's shoreline. A white lobster boat with a red stripe across its hull and cockpit moved slowly across the horizon as the two-man crew pulled their pots from the Atlantic floor.

Joseph Alfonse Bonnato's funeral drew more people than Eve could count. At the church the governor, Director of the FBI, and both Massachusetts Senators were among the number of people who spoke glowingly and reverently about the man and his legacy of service and sacrifice. The priest at St. Anne's also read a warm and poignant note from President Olson.

Eve had worked with Joe off and on for more than a dozen years, ever since the Boston Marathon bombing—which was assigned to her by the CIA and brought her to the city that she now calls home. Since Joe was from Boston, he took that bombing very personally.

He's the one who tracked down the Tsarnaev brothers. He shot the older brother in an exchange of gunfire as the two fled, which caused the younger to drag the older brother with the car some distance as he made his getaway.

Joe then headed up tracking the remaining brother down. Plucked Tsarnaev from his hiding place in a boat parked in a Watertown resident's driveway. It's one of the reasons he rose so quickly to become the FBI's Boston SAC (Special Agent in Charge) at such a young age. And it forever forged his reputation, especially among the law enforcement community.

Eve considered Joe one of her closest friends. And she was one of the last people to see and speak to him before his death at the hand of John Trahison's missile that disintegrated so many people that ill-fated day a year ago, now known as the Greater Boston Massacre. Yet she was still surprised by how much she learned about Joe's life and history from those who eulogized him.

Joe's grandfather immigrated to the States from Italy in 1935 and settled in Gloucester, Massachusetts with his young wife. He got a job working on a lobster boat and became a U.S. citizen two years later. He joined the Marines in 1941 after the Japanese bombed Pearl Harbor to eagerly fight for his newly adopted country. He saw more than his share of action in Guadalcanal the following year, earning the Navy Cross and two Purple Hearts. This told Eve a lot about the man. She knew what those medals meant and the price he had to pay to earn them.

Joe's father followed suit, and at the age of 18 joined the Marines during the Vietnam war. He spent nearly all of his in-country tour in Khe Sanh, along with six thousand other Marines who were there to interdict the enemy's flow of supplies on the Ho Chi Minh Trail.

Like his father before him, he also distinguished himself during the fierce battles that took place, when three divisions of the People's Army of North Vietnam and some Viet Cong, more than 20,000 men, launched an assault on the base that lasted for five months. Joe's father was also awarded the Navy Cross.

Eve was beginning to gain a clearer picture of the cloth that her good friend was cut from.

When Joe's grandfather returned from the war, with the help of a G.I. Bill loan, he purchased his own lobster boat. His diligent work ethic and natural business instincts led to his purchasing two more boats and then starting a thriving live-lobster delivery business that Joe's father continued to expand into what is today one of the largest seafood wholesale operations in New England.

Joe, however, chose not to continue the family's Marine legacy after college and instead joined the Army, becoming a Green Beret. He, like Eve, spent his entire tour of duty in Afghanistan. He also broke with the tradition of becoming part of the family business once completing his service, and instead pursued a career with the FBI, leaving the management and expansion of the family seafood empire in the extremely capable hands of his sister, the company's current CEO. Eve could see her standing on the other side of Joe's gravesite, next to Joe's wife and their three teenage children.

Joe was joining his grandfather and father today, being laid to rest in the same veterans' lot of the cemetery where they are also interred. Although with one notable difference—while the same simple white crosses stood as sentinels over their earthly remains, Joe's flag-draped coffin was empty. The raging, gas-fueled fire cloud that reached 2,600-degrees Fahrenheit left no remains of him and all who were with him. They were instantly reduced to ashen dust that sank to the bottom of the Mystic River.

If there was any comfort, Eve thought, it was that she doubted Joe even knew what hit him. It all happened so quickly and so overwhelmingly. She recalled when they were about to board the boats that would take him to the LNG tanker that was hit by the missile and her to the Long Island lighthouse, the source of Trahison's missile launch. As they were donning their gear, she asked Joe why he wasn't putting on any body armor and he replied, "Will it stop a three-thousand-degree fireball?" She never for a moment thought the question would actually be answered when she replied, "Let's hope it never comes to that."

But it had come to that.

Joe and those with him were among the first of the more than half million people killed that June day and, in the days, weeks and months that followed.

Eve wondered how many funerals like this had been held over the last year, funerals without bodies or even ashes to bury. Or how many thousands of funerals were never held, or will ever be held, because there are no family members left alive to bury their dead. Entire cities and family lineages had been completely obliterated. Erased. Expunged from existence, but not from recorded memory.

Nearly all had left digital footprints that can be followed, embedded on the memory chips of federal, state, and local government databases, email and social media servers—records of each life's significant events reduced to caches and clouds of ones and zeros.

As taps began to play, Eve recalled the many times that she and Joe talked about their experiences in Afghanistan, at least as much as she could divulge given the top-secret nature of most of her work there. She missed these.

Sharing Afghanistan was one of the strongest bonds of their friendship. And talking about it was cathartic for both, especially for Eve, since there were so few people she was close to in Boston and even fewer to whom she could open up to about any of it.

Retelling and now safely reliving their experiences, especially the most horrific ones, took away some of the power these memories held. Bringing them into the light, examining and unfolding them in their telling, helped to loosen their grip on the darkest corners of their minds. Forgetting these past experiences was impossible. But removing their hold on the present was not.

They met once after work at Bar Mezzana on Harrison Avenue and liked it so much that this became the place for what evolved into a monthly hangout for almost two years before the Trahison situation started heating up. The Mezzana was just a couple of blocks away from Eve's loft and a few blocks down the street from the District D-4 police station where the Homeland team met.

They typically sat at the same table near the bar. And when the weather was warm, they shared a table on the outdoor patio. Eve was quite partial to their eggplant rollatini, and Joe loved their lamb meatballs. Both drank their bourbon neat.

As the bugler playing Taps finished and the priest began his encomium, Eve's mind drifted to one of the many times they met there. While working on their second drink and waiting for their food to arrive, she asked Joe, "What surprised you most when you first got to 'Stan?"

"We were part of Operation Dagger. Right after 9/11. First ones in. None of us had a clue. We didn't know the Afghan weather could change so drastically from one mile to the next. We went from a sandstorm to black-sky rain, to hail, then snow and ice, all within 48 hours. We were completely unprepared and miserable. You?"

"First time in Kabul. Definitely the smell. I'll never forget the unmistakable bouquet of burning tires, rotting garbage, and Middle Eastern spices."

He frowned. "Incredible how many memories smells can trigger, isn't it? For me it's charred hair, cordite, and gunpowder… You in Kabul a lot?"

"Early on it was Taliban central. At least until the Northern Alliance marched in in November that second year and the Taliban skedaddled without firing a shot. It was one of the few places where being a woman was a clear advantage. Women are invisible in that culture, especially in a crowded city like Kabul. Same in Kandahar later."

She took a sip of her bourbon. "With my brown hair, although little of that could be seen under my headscarf, my hazel eyes, and being five-foot-five, just a couple inches taller than most Afghan women, I could be invisible, too. And I often went full burka—talk about hiding in plain sight. I was able to serve the mission well. Particularly in the early months."

"Spill deets."

"Spill deets… Really? she asked."

"What, too much? My daughter says I'm not hip. So, I'm working on it."

"Okay, Dr. Evil."

"Huh?"

"Austin Powers? 'I'm hip. I'm with it.' You've seen it?"

"That bad huh?"

Smiling, she added, "Worse. How old is Meghan now?"

"Twelve."

"Yikes. Now the fun starts."

"Tell me about it."

"See, now that right there would have been a better response than 'spill deets.' More you."

"Sure. But not very cool."

"Real cool doesn't try to be cool. It just is."

"That's why I'll never be cool to Meghan."

"Trust me. In time she'll discover how *cool* you really are. Just keep doing you."

"*That* I can do… So, Kabul."

"Well, it's now public knowledge that the CIA had been developing networks of sources in Afghanistan for twenty years prior to 9/11. So, we were already armed with plenty of critical information on the enemy's capabilities, intentions, motivations, and plans. It's the reason your operation, Dagger, and nearly all of the other early ops were so successful so quickly."

Holding up his glass and tipping it toward Eve, "Well, thank you, then."

Tapping her glass to his she said, "Sorry we couldn't do anything about the miserable weather, though."

"So, you were also in-country early?"

"Yup. Just over four weeks after the attack. Like you I found myself nine time zones and eight thousand miles away from home."

He nodded. "The terrain was so different. Other worldly. Those towering rock formations. Hindu Kush mountains and valleys. The Baba range. Lush trees, thick woods and vegetation by the rivers. Then to the west, the Kandahar plains, just the opposite. Zilch. Vast, dreary, bare rocks and ridges. Nothing but browns and tans and big and little rocks everywhere you looked. Even the rising sun was a different shade of red. Did it all surprise you like it did me?”

“It did. But oddly enough I was also inspired by it. Fascinated actually. Those colors now show up in my paintings quite often.”

“So, you must speak Dari then?”

“Eh, so-so. My Dari is passable. Picked up some Pashto, as well.”

“Could have used you when working with all those warlords as we started the Northern Alliance. As you noted, once formed, it didn’t take long for the US to lose any real control over them. So many tribes, so many different languages. Something like forty spoken in a country the size of Texas. It was nuts! Or majnun, as they say in Arabic. A few of us spoke some Arabic, a couple knew some Farsi and one or two some Russian. Giant pain in the ass doing three-way translations to communicate even the simplest things. You alone in Kabul?”

“The only woman. But no, not alone. I had a Joint Task Force 2 team. My JTF2 team and some SEAL, Delta, MARSOC, and Green Beret teams were part of the Agency’s Directorate of Support. And my group included a couple of local assets.”

Joe noticed her face go blank. He knew that thousand-yard stare all too well and after a few moments, said, “Hey, where did you just go?”

“Ah, sorry… Mentioning locals on the team put me back there.”

Grinning, “Spill deets.”

“Had a bead on a high-level Taliban leader. We knew where he was staying that night. Aziz, one of my locals, who had helped track and take out three others, betrayed us this time. House was booby trapped. The IED took out three of my team and nearly killed me. The guy directly in front of me, Victor Watts, a

SEAL, took the brunt of the blast. When I woke, I was wearing most of him. Spent three months in ICU.

"Internal organs swelled so much, they had to cut me open from here to here." Pointing from her breastbone to her crotch. "Had to leave me open until everything returned to normal, which took more than a month. Kept me in a chemical-induced coma."

"Shit. That sucks."

"Yup. But I'm still here. Too many others can't say that. Including Lieutenant Watts."

Lifting his glass, Joe said, "Here's to Lieutenant Watts and all those who gave everything they had."

Clinking glasses, Eve said, "May they rest in power."

"Ever catch up with Aziz?"

"Couple members of my team tracked him two days later. Took him out in an alley in Marjan Town. Dropped him on a pile of garbage."

"Don't ya' just love justice when it's poetic."

"Once I got back from the hospital and rehab a couple of months later, we picked up where we left off and finally snatched n' grabbed that same Taliban leader. Tracked him to Pakistan. Turns out he was a linchpin to Al-Qaeda, to a Pakistani Islamist group, and to the Islamic Movement of Uzbekistan. A huge score. Squeezed lots of intel out of him. What about you, what rings your bell at three in the morning?"

"That's easy. One of my missions in the Arghandab River Valley."

"Heard about the Valley. Never there myself. I read that invaders been having their asses handed to them there since Alexander the Great."

"Why it's called the 'meat grinder.' Like you, we got intel on a big Taliban mucky muck. Scoped his house. Confirmed he was there. It was one of those Afghan compounds you see all over the place—outer stone and cement and mud walls surrounding inner flat-roofed buildings. This was a smaller one. Looked like it had been abandoned for years. Lots of overgrown vegetation. Some animals even moved in. Made it the ideal hiding place for a few nights. Don't have to tell you the insurgents were masters of IED creation and placement."

"Nope. Got the scars to prove it."

"So much ordinance got left behind by the Russians, these guys became wizzes at repurposing that stuff into smaller anti-personnel mines. The night we went in, standard team of twelve with Sergeant Dix, one of my engineers on lead with the mine detector. He cleared the path and wall all the way to the door. The two behind him joined up and the third, Sergeant Marshall, walking the same path, stepped on a toe popper that was daisy chained to a large charge in the wall."

"Shit. The detector missed it?" she asked.

"Bastards used what's called a 'hockey puck' initiator. No more metal than a pin in it. And the soil had such high iron content, the initiator and the charge were completely masked."

"That iron soil was just about everywhere in 'Stan. Really fucked with radio comms. So, how bad?"

"Marshall was pink-misted and dismembered. Pieces of him went everywhere. I was in the back, knocked on my ass by the shock wave. A few who were closer were tossed like rag dolls twenty or so yards. A couple wounded pretty badly. Airlifted them out. Some broken bones. Dislocations. A few concussions. No other fatalities. Could have been much worse.

"Watched Marshall come apart in slow motion. Plays like a movie in my head most nights… Some nights I'm the one coming apart… We put what we could find of him in a body bag. Alive he was about 185. All that was left weighed about forty, maybe fifty pounds."

"Shit… Get your bad guy?"

"Yup. One was taken out by their own IED when it went off. He was on the other side of the wall. We went in through the hole and leveled the three buildings with M72's. Cut down anything that still moved. ID'd our Taliban target with a photo. Ten bad guys total. Turns out two others were also high on the hit list."

After the priest finished speaking and the widow was handed the tri-folded flag by a saluting Beret, family members took turns placing flowers on her friend's empty casket and began to leave. Eve held back and was among the last to place her flower. The crowd had already thinned greatly. She had said her goodbyes to her good friend countless times over the last year, every time she thought of him, so she simply placed her hand on the coffin for a few moments and quietly spoke the last thing he had said to her, "See you on the flip side."

As she began to walk away, lost in thought, a familiar voice came from behind her. "Well, hey there stranger."

Eve turned and after a beat, smiled brightly and hugged Captain Bill Evans, Boston D-4 Police Station's commanding officer and her co-leader on the city's Homeland Security team. "Well, hey there yourself! I was wondering if I'd see you here. Almost didn't recognize you in your dress blues. La-de-da. It's a good look on you."

"Sure. I'm a regular chick magnet. It's why I don't wear them very often. Don't want to upset too many of Boston's menfolk."

They walked together out of the cemetery's veterans section entrance, past the time-worn tombstones dating back to the sixteenth century. They came to the Fisherman's Last Port of Call memorial, a fenced-in field of stubby headstones surrounding an impressive granite block with a huge ship's anchor, painted white, resting on top, its thick chain descended one side and wrapped around the granite base. Eve paused to read the inscription:

> *These lads have joined the silent majority and*
> *here lie in peace*
> *where no wind or wave can disturb their rest.*
> *Charmed by the sea*
> *they fought many a gale with a courage and*
> *fortitude typical*
> *of Gloucester fishermen.*

As they made their way toward the parking lot, Bill asked, "Are you back here for good or is this just a visit."

"Still in DC. But will definitely be moving back to Boston. Hopefully in the near future."

"I know we've spoken a couple of times since you've been away, but I want to reiterate once again that the team and I are at your beckon call."

"Thanks, Bill. I was actually going to call you. There's one thing you can help me with while I'm here."

"Name it."

"Hunter's apartment is still secured, yes?"

"Yup. Just as he left it. We've not gotten the go-ahead to release it yet."

"That's because of me. I'd like to see it tomorrow, if that's okay."

"Just say when. I'll come with."

"Perfect. How are the two Dicks doing?" She was referencing

detectives Dick Murphy and Dick Sweeney, stationed with Evans at D-4 and fellow members of Boston's Homeland team, along with the late Bonnato and the late and later-revealed turncoat, Hunter Forte.

"They're actually around here somewhere." Doing a quick scan. "Hard to tell among all this blue, though. They're crazy as ever. For the most part. Murphy's a bit more subdued. Took a big family and friends hit when the fire wiped Everett off the map. But he and Sweeney still trade badly clichéd wife and mother jabs with regularity."

"Never thought I'd miss those terrible jokes as much as I do."

"They'll be delighted to see you, I'm sure. Where you staying, if not in your loft?"

"I'm not quite ready to deal with the ghosts there. I'm staying with an old friend who lives here in Gloucester. Right up the road, in fact. Brice Howland. A fellow artist I've known for years. His work is also represented by the Newbury Gallery."

"Lot of ghosts everywhere, these days."

Eve got to her car, stopped and stood facing Bill. "Let's catch up some more tomorrow. I'll come by around nine, if that works for you."

After one last hug he said, "See you then."

Chapter 2

Eve had trouble finding a parking spot on Harrison Avenue near the District D-4 Police Station, typical for the South End, and one of the reasons she doesn't own or want a car when she lives here. Even the station's lot was full. So, she went one block further north and found an empty metered spot on Wareham Street, directly across from #59. It was a Civil War era, five-story brick building that housed about 40 artists, a few of whom she knew well, since they were also represented by Newbury Gallery and had been in several group exhibits with her.

She had been in the building numerous times. Usually, to visit one of her close friends, Esther Garcia Eder. She and Esther met a few years ago at a group show in which they both had work and formed a nearly instant friendship. Eve was drawn to her loose, colorful landscapes, seascapes, and portraits that Eve thought had an echo of Matisse and Bonnard.

Because it was only four blocks from Eve's studio, they'd meet for coffee in Esther's sunny, west-facing studio at couple times a month to discuss the art that each had been working on, the art books they just purchased, their families, and whatever else each had going on in their lives. At least as much as Eve could share that wasn't CIA or Homeland related.

So whenever Esther would leave for the summer to live and

work in her home and studio on an island in Maine, Eve would miss their coffee clutches and eagerly anticipate her return in time for the annual Open Studios event held in this area, known as the SOWA arts district, every September. Eve knew Esther was in Maine now and reminded herself to reach out to her dear friend as soon as she returned to DC.

After feeding the meter, she headed back to Harrison, went left one block to Plympton Street, which cornered the police station. As soon as she entered the station's front door under its large, arched-windowed entrance, a rush of déjà vu sights, smells, sounds, and emotions hit her like a wall. It surprised her, but it also made sense.

It had been a year since she was here last. This building, mostly its third-floor conference room—where Boston's Homeland Security team met monthly for a few years and then nearly every day for more than a year leading up to the Greater Boston Massacre—had essentially become her second home. And the guys she was about to see had become her second family.

As she entered the conference room, not much had changed. The same map of Boston and the harbor was attached to a white board on one wall. The flat screen monitor still sat above the credenza that held the coffee pot, cups, stirrers and an unopened box of donuts, cliché be damned. The smell of the freshly brewed pot called to her. At the other end of the room, a large, arched window took up most of the wall and looked out onto Harrison Avenue—to the right, the spired top of the Holy Cross Cathedral poked above the surrounding houses and apartment buildings, a sacred sentinel watching over the neighborhood.

The only addition to the room made while she had been away was on the wall opposite the map. It was completely filled with thumbtacked and taped newspaper clippings, end-to-end and floor to ceiling, mostly from the *Boston Globe* and all of them related to the Greater Boston Massacre.

They created a timeline of the event with headlines and photos: *LNG GAS EXPLOSION! THOUSANDS KILLED! / MANY THOUSANDS OF LIVES LOST IN MOMENTS / UNPRECENDENTED DEATH & DESTRUCTION / FIRES STILL RAGING / ACCIDENT OR TERRORIST ATTACK? / ENTIRE CITIES DESTROYED! / MANY THOUSANDS STILL MISSING, ASSUMED DEAD. / TERRORISTS ATTACK BOSTON WITH MISSILES! / HELP ARRIVES FROM ALL OVER NATION & WORLD / THE GREATER BOSTON MASSACRE: MORE DEAD THAN HIROSHIMA AND NAGASAKI / PRESIDENT ADDRESSES BOSTON AND NATION / FIRES OUT. SEARCH FOR INJURED AND DEAD CONTINUES. / COULD GREATER BOSTON MASSACRE HAVE BEEN PREVENTED? / GREATER BOSTON MASSACRE CONSPIRACY REVEALED / LATE SENATOR TRAHISON AND NEPHEW BEHIND GREATER BOSTON MASSACRE / WHO ELSE INVOLVED IN GREATER BOSTON MASSACRE CONSPIRACY?*

"Who else indeed," she said as she moved from left to right, scanning the more recent clippings. One issue of the *Sunday Globe* had a multi-page magazine section dedicated to the tragedy listing every person who was confirmed dead or unaccounted for. She skimmed the pages of seemingly endless lists of names, recorded by city, totaling just over six hundred thousand souls, and then read the most recent newspaper headlines: *DNA RECOVERY EFFORT ENDS / GOVENOR APPOINTS GREATER BOSTON MASSACRE MEMORIAL COMMITTEE.*

Captain Bill Evans and Detectives Dick Murphy and Dick Sweeney entered the conference room. "Whada sight for sowah eyes you ah!" Murphy bellowed, as he quickly went to her and gave her a big hug. After they embraced, Eve held his shoulders, looked up at him directly in the eyes and said, "I'm so sorry for your losses, Dick. Your family. Your friends… Your city. I wish— "

Eyes welling. Quietly. "Thanks, Eve… Helps a little ta know ya gawt the bastid."

After Eve hugged Dick Sweeney and Captain Evans, Sweeney said, "We got some details of what went down in the lighthouse, but not much. Hoping you can fill us in."

Eve went to the credenza to pour some coffee and said, "Sure. Let's take a load off and I'll spill the deets, as Bonnato once said to me, what seems a lifetime ago."

"Dat was some send off, wasnnit? Purfekly fittin' a hero," Murphy added.

No one said anything for a couple of minutes, each contemplating their own memories of the man who was their colleague and their friend. Eve broke the silence. "I still beat myself up for his death. Silly, I know. But still…"

"You can't do that," Evans said. "The Trahisons did it all. And no one caught on to Hunter. Even as close as you two were."

"I know. Hopefully, when we head over to his apartment we'll discover something we can use to find any other treasonous bastards involved. Where were we?"

"The lighthouse," Sweeney said.

"Before we get into that," pointing to the headline, "tell me about the Memorial Committee. What's being planned, do you know?"

Evans said, "After a year of an army of people working day and night to gather as much DNA as they could, the effort had been continually thwarted by the weather. The seven-mile radius of destruction is simply too large to cover effectively. So, every time it rains, or snows, or the wind picks up—and it does a lot of all that around here as you know—the mounds of ash have been incessantly compromised. So much has been washed away, mixed together or carried off into the sky, and it became apparent that it will be impossible to positively identify everyone who was lost. So now local, state, and federal records are being data mined with the help of AI algorithms to identify the lost and locate any potential living relatives.

"As a result, the resolution that everyone seems to be leaning toward is to gather the remaining tons of ash from the entire expanse of destruction. Truck it all to a massive, deep rectangular hole, about the size of four city blocks, that's to be dug at ground zero, much like the foundations of the World Trade Center's twin towers in New York.

"It will have multi-tiered walls, steps, ramps and landings, sort of like an inverted Aztec temple." Holding it up, "Here's an artist's rendering in a recent *Globe* article that we haven't added to the wall yet. The ash will be mixed into the concrete used to build it. A temporary concrete-making operation was already built on site. Every one of the more than six hundred thousand names will be etched into the stained, highly polished concrete walls. And an eternal flame will burn at the base in the center."

"Wow." Eve said, nearly whispering, "What an incredible solution and tribute."

Evans added, "A Boston architect and sculptor worked together to come up with the idea and plans. Legislators approved the budget. Governor just signed off. It's gonna start very soon."

Teary eyed, Eve got up to pour more coffee—even though her cup was still nearly full—to compose herself, trying not to lose it completely and break down crying. Her back to them, she wiped her eyes with a napkin and turned, forcing a smile as she sat back down. "Okay… the lighthouse. Well, you probably already know we had two Maryland State officers with us, Lieutenant D'agastino and Sergeant Bagarella. You would've liked them." Pointing to Sweeney and Murphy. "In many ways they reminded me of you guys. Italian versions."

"I'm half Italian," Sweeney said. "Mother's side."

"Dat must be the side I like," Murphy injected.

Eve continued. "Unfortunately, I didn't know Hunter planned to assassinate them as soon as we had Trahison bagged and on the floor."

"That when he shot you in the foot?" Evans asked.

"Yup. He made Trahison carry the missiles to the top of the lighthouse. With me following. I was pretty sure he wasn't going to have Trahison blow up the LNG facility and light up the nuclear power plant and rain hell on Washington D.C. He knew there was an array of Patriot missiles set up at NAS Pax River to stop that from happening. And with the senator's bill and hidden agenda already laid bare, it would no longer serve any purpose. His plan was to kill us both. Blame Trahison for my death and the troopers' and fly off in the Gulfstream. Said he had a plan to disappear. Funny… he said he was about to hurtle off into the night sky and become a ghost. He was right on both counts, just not the way he intended."

"Fuckum. Good riddance," Murphy said.

"Much of what happened was in the news. That the senator's heart attack was caused by poison. His chief of staff was responsible and was executed in his car shortly after. Hunter's role in the poisoning, the cabal, and his double cross. Something else you didn't know, Hunter actually told Trevor Brock, Trahison's chief of staff, that what he was putting in the senator's coffee would only knock him out. Had no clue it was lethal. Poor stupid kid… The spotlight that all of this put on you guys was pretty intense, wasn't it?"

Evans said, "We put the BPD's Office of Public Relations on it. It's why they get the big bucks. Their department head, Randy Labonte, ran interference for us. Became our face and voice. Kept us out of it. So far, so good."

Sweeney said, "News and social media are rife with a crazy array of conspiracy theories. Everything from the Democrats did it so they can hold it over the Republicans, to the Russians working with the Pope. From the Iranians and mind-controlled sharks to the Deep State and Disney being behind it all. I kid you not. I'm surprised no one's claimed it was Serleena the Kylothian." To their puzzled looks. "From the *Men in Black* movies. Seriously though, Congress is talking about starting inquiries. Issuing subpoenas."

Eve said, "I heard. And that reporters have been looking for Elise Wainwright, the alias I used when I met with the senator. Why we're trying to move quickly. Once we nail the other conspirators, the president will at the very least inform senior members of the Senate's Select Intelligence Committee. He may even address the nation, but that will depend on how all of this unfolds. Either way, we in this room and others in DC will work hard over the next weeks and months to put all of this to bed. Hopefully not too many months.

"Here's more of what you don't yet know. The president met with Hunter and me after the senator died in my hands. Told us the autopsy results, the poison in the senator's coffee and his chief of staff being shot dead in his car. After our White House meeting ended, he asked me to stay behind. That's when he told me that Hunter was part of the conspiracy. Showed me a transcript of a phone conversation Hunter had with Trevor and some others at phone numbers we've not yet identified. He and Trevor talked about meeting up at a certain time and place and that Hunter would be giving him something to incapacitate the senator for the meeting he would be having with me the next morning. I'm pretty sure Hunter made that call during our meeting here in this conference room, one of the times he went out into the hallway."

Murphy said, "Sonofabitch!"

"Also, when I told you guys that the CIA had decided to secretly wiretap the senator's phones, at that time you may recall I also mentioned that there were a couple of other things we were doing that I couldn't discuss. One of them was we thought it made sense to also listen in on the phones of those closest to him, Trevor and his executive assistant, Cheryl Smokler."

"I can only imagine how hard it was for you to not want to take Hunter out right then and there," Evans said.

"Oh, you have no idea. I almost put blanks in his weapons when packing our stuff to head to the Hooper Island lighthouse. I should have. And I regret it."

"You made the right call." Sweeney said. "If he discovered it beforehand, you'd be dead. Besides, there's no way you could have known he was going to take out the troopers. Don't beat yourself up.

"Thanks, Dick. What wasn't in the released reports was how Hunter and Trahison went down."

"Evans said, "News said they shot each other."

"Half right. Trahison got Hunter. Had a small .32-caliber wrapped to his wounded leg that we never saw. Shot him in the neck when he made his move to take out Trahison. Hunter dropped onto the lighthouse's platform, his MP-5 caught the railing, and the strap hung him there by the neck. He was already dead. Coroner said one of the bullets severed his brain stem."

"Shit," Murphy said. "But a fittin' end, I mus say. So, you got Trahison then?"

"Yup. He shot me once. Vest stopped it. Never got off a second. Nearly broke his wrist disarming him. Emptied his gun into him. Heat of the moment decision."

Evans said, "We would've done the same. The fact that you were never mentioned in the news seems to be end of story for you."

Eve said, "So far, at least. Not sure how long that will last, though. President Olson has kept a very tight lid on the more delicate details so far. Only one Top Secret report mentions me and my role. It's an 'Eyes Only' file, so only three or four people outside of us know all the facts."

Evans said, "Congress seems to be weeks, perhaps months away from starting any hearings. They can't even agree on where, when, or who to start with."

Eve said, "With what I'm doing in DC and your help, the goal is to have all of their questions answered before they even ask them."

Sweeney said, "So what are you looking for in Hunter's apartment?"

"There was no burner phone on Hunter's body. He obviously had one. Thought it may have dropped into the Chesapeake when he fell. Divers found nothing. A sweep of the jet also came up empty. I think it may still be in his apartment, hidden somewhere. Hoping we can find it and any other leads we can use to help identify the rest. Another senator, a Supreme Court Justice, and someone in the president's inner circle. Facts known only to a select few, which now includes you guys."

"A fuckin' Supreme?" Murphy said. "Damn."

Evans added, "What about Hunter's boss, Alex Marshall, Secretary of Homeland? Seems a likely inner-circle candidate to me."

Eve said, "I asked Hunter that very question in the lighthouse. Said Alex Marshall never had a clue. The president was relieved. And Alex has been working with us in the background."

"As always, all of this is knowledge that will never leave this room," Evans said. "And we'll work with you on our end. Whatever you need, we're on it."

Murphy said, "Heah, heah" at the same time Sweeney said, "Absolutely."

"Thanks guys. I'll probably take you up on that. I've been unpacking this with the president for the last few months. Looking at every senator. Every justice. Lots of speculating about his inner circle. So far, nothing solid. Time to work it from this end."

"Well, let's head over there. See what we can see," Evans said. As they stood, he added. "Sweeney, I know you've got that witness interview for the Albertson murder case, so the three of us'll cover this."

"Happy hunting at Hunter's," Sweeney said. Evans and Eve groaned nearly in unison.

Murphy said, "Don quit yowah day job, buddy. Aaron Sorkin (pronounced Ahrin Sawkin) you ain't."

Chapter 3

The Jones apartment complex is on East Dedham Street, one of the streets that corners the D-4 Police Station. It was a three-minute walk to the modern, high-end, u-shaped, six-story building that housed 650 studio, single-, and double-bedroom apartments, with rents ranging from three to ten grand a month.

As Eve, Evans and Murphy walked into the lobby, noting the highly polished marble floors, a long row of round marble coffee tables surrounded by opulent leather chairs, the huge floor-to-ceiling windows throughout the highly lofted space, a white brick wall with a fifteen-foot long, four-foot tall gas fireplace, generous wood and stone accents all over, and erudite abstract art hanging on the walls throughout, Murphy whistled and said, "Fuck me. I'm joinin' Homeland, Cap'n. Nuthin' personal. But Bawston cleahly ain't gowt anywheah neah Fed budgets. Tawk abowt livin' da high life."

"I won't stop ya. One less pain in my ass is all."

"Definitely tempted… but I can't. I'd hate da make Sweeney cry. He's Laurel to my Hahdy."

"More like Bill to your Ted."

"I was thinking Statler and Waldorf," Eve said. To their blank looks, "The old-men Muppet hecklers." They were all chuckling as they entered the elevator, and Eve hit the fourth-floor button. Once the elevator door closed, each pulled on a pair of surgical gloves.

Eve pulled a key from her pocket as she led them down the hall to apartment number 432 and opened the door. The space was bright and airy. White walls, high white ceiling reflected the light emitted by two south-facing walls of floor-to-ceiling windows at the other end of the open-loft floor plan. "All right, gentlemen," she said. "Let's be thorough. Murphy, you can take this closet. Bathroom's behind you and the kitchen's down the hall on the left. Captain, the bedroom's down the hall to the right and it has a walk-in closet. I'll go through the closet near the living room and then the living room itself. Shout if you find anything."

Eve went down the hall and opened the closet door. The first thing she noticed was Hunter's leather bomber jacket on a hanger. It was from his Navy days as an F/A-18 Super Hornet pilot in Afghanistan. And it brought back a conflagration of memories and feelings, mostly of the first night they spent together, the beginning of their passionate, seemingly flourishing year-long relationship. She was as certain as she had ever been that she was in love. And just as certain he was, too.

She started thinking the same thoughts she'd been wrestling with for the past year: *How could I have been so wrong? All the right signs were there. All the boxes ticked. How the hell am I ever going to trust my gut about intimate relationships again?*

She thought she had finally conquered her demons, the ones that kept telling her that no one would want her beyond a physical fling because she was so broken. Such damaged goods. That Afghanistan had done a number on her. Left her emotionally unavailable. Distant. Restrained.

All that was beginning to change with Hunter. Like skin

gradually shed without her being aware until noticing it was simply gone.

As things had moved along so well with Hunter, just before it all went tits up, she was just beginning to think that perhaps she was finally done with her default, go-to defensive move of ending a relationship as soon as someone got too close. Calling it quits before her brokenness was fully exposed. Beating him to the punch that she was certain would be coming. Employing offense as defense.

But she was now pretty much back to square one. Finding solace once again in shutting down emotionally. Turning inward. Reverting to an old go-to thought. A thought she knew that a shrink would have a field day with: *To be willing to take a bullet wound over a heart wound any day of the week.*

There was something to be said for being self-contained. Self-fulfilled. She didn't need a mate to complete her. *Sharing life with someone else may or may not be off the table for me. It's not like I lack centeredness or lose my balance when I'm alone. Perhaps there's someone out there with strengths and weaknesses that compliment mine, and mine his. So long as he's not a cold-blooded murderer who was part of a secret cabal that obliterated more than six-hundred thousand innocent people. Been there, done that. Meanwhile, I'm not—* Her musings were interrupted by Captain Evans calling from the bedroom.

"Hey, guys, think I have something here."

Eve and Murphy joined Evans in the bedroom's walk-in closet. She said, "Whatcha got?"

"I went to turn on this light switch and not only did nothing happen, it feels all loosey-goosey, like it isn't even connected to anything." Shining his small flashlight on it. "And here. The screws and plate are scratched and well worn. Like it's seen a lot of use. Anyone got a screwdriver?"

Eve said, "There's one in the kitchen drawer. I'll get it."

She handed it to Evans, and he removed the two screws holding the switch plate, then the plate itself. Unscrewed the toggle screws and pulled. Two wires normally attached to each side of the switch—the live and ground wires—were unattached, bent away and pushed to the sides. But a single black wire was attached to the base of the switch, wrapped around the bottom screw hole, and as he pulled out about a foot of wire, tied to the end was a cell phone.

"Fuck me," Murphy said. "Tricky bastid."

Eve said, "Captain, you must be a clairvoyant mystic."

"Nope, just a cop." As he hands her the phone, "Wanna see my flat feet?"

Smiling broadly. "Again with the feet? You made the same offer a year ago, as I recall. I'm still good, thanks… Where's the battery? It should be somewhere nearby."

Murphy went to the nightstand next to the bed and opened the drawer. "Well, looky, looky," he said as he held up the battery and handed it to Eve.

She said, "Perfect. We'll find out what's on this when I get back to DC. Let's keep looking. We're on a roll, gentlemen!"

A half hour later, Murphy and Evans came into the living room. A nut-brown saddle-leather, L-shaped sofa with short metal legs took up much of the space in front of one of the corner floor-to-ceiling windows. A glass-topped coffee table in front of it. To the left, in front of the other window, a blue-linen Vail chair held a small tan throw pillow. Evans said, "We tossed the place. Didn't find anything else."

On the right side of the room, in front of the other corner windows, Eve was sitting in a desk chair going through some opened and saved mail she removed from a chrome rack that sat on top of a small marble desk. "This is odd. In the middle of this stack. He's got not one, but two envelopes from a landscaping company, Earthworks Lawn Care, a PO Box address."

"What's he need a lanscapah foh in dis place?" Murphy said.

"Exactly." As she pulled out one of the letters, "Where else have I seen something like this? Shit. I can't recall." She scanned and read aloud. "We do quality yard work, blah, blah, blah. Ah… We will be in your area on Friday, February 2nd, between the hours of 2:00 to 3:00 pm. We would love to tell you more and provide you with a free estimate for our services." She dropped it onto the desk and removed the letter from the other envelope. "Same letter copy except for different dates and times…

"Shit! I remember where I saw this before! Senator Trahison's desk. After he died, I was interviewed for a couple of hours, answering the same questions from Capital and DC Metro cops and detectives. We sat in the chairs in front of his desk. Among some papers and folders on top of a blotter, he had one of these envelopes tucked into the blotter's corner. I'm sure of it."

Evans, looking over her shoulder, said, "The date and time. Must be how they're notified to turn on their burners."

"Exactly what I was thinking, Bill."

"Fuckin' ay," said Murphy. "Hidden in plain sight."

"Not anymore," said Eve.

Chapter 4

The fire snapped off several rapid shots, spitting a trail of orange and yellow sparks into the night sky. Brice had just added another log to the roaring fire pit, a four-foot circle of gray granite fieldstones stacked two-feet high, and said, "Oooh. I guess that one still had some sap!" as he sat back down in a weathered, green, wooden Adirondack chair to the left of Eve.

"It's truly a beautiful place you have here, Brice. Thank you again for hosting me. And after a meal like that, I may decide to never leave!"

He took a sip from his glass of Guinness and licked the tan foam from the bottom of the moustache of his white goatee. His round, wire-framed glasses—arched by white, wild and wooly eyebrows—reflected the dancing flames as he placed his beer on the chair's flat armrest and replied, "You're welcome to stay at the Howland hacienda for as long as you like. We've certainly got the room. And we do miss the company. Kids have been gone for years now. Never thought I'd long for the chaos and noise as much as I do. It's great when they all visit with the grandkids, though."

"How many grandchildren do you and Elise have now?"

"Nine."

"Wow! That's a houseful."

"We love it."

Across the long, downward slopping, tightly mowed lawn, bracketed by tall white pines, red oak, river birch, and striped maple trees, the waxing, not-quite-full moon glinted across the undulating ocean surface and danced with the waves rolling onto the rocks two hundred yards away. Eve asked, "How long have you guys been living in this little slice of heaven?"

"Over forty years now."

"Really? The house looks so new."

"Because it is. Had a fire about ten years ago. Lightning strike. Most of the house went up. Total loss. Had to knock down what little was left standing. No one was hurt, thank God. But I did lose about two hundred paintings. My studio was on the top floor, the exact spot where the lightning struck. On the upside, I got to design the ideal northern sky-lighted painting studio and Elise got the open living space and fieldstone fireplace she'd always wanted."

"Lightning? Two hundred paintings? Shit!... That's harsh."

Chuckling. "Yup… Bet you didn't know God was an art critic."

"I know you're kidding but also somewhat serious about that, aren't you? I know how much your faith means. One of the things I admire about you. That and your exquisite paintings, of course. You taught at Gordon, right? It's Christian?"

"First, thank you. You know I'm a big fan of your work, too. It's so emotive. I love how you leave room for the accident to be part of the creative process. And yes, Gordon's a Christian college. Taught there thirty-five years. And yeah, the fire actually did cause a lot of internal reflection on my part. How could it not? *Struck by lightning* is a cliché for God's judgment for a reason, right? That's actually why I didn't give it much thought at first.

"But I couldn't shake the sense that came with it. More than a feeling. A knowing. That started a lot of wrestling with God. A lot of reflecting. Scripture reading. Soul searching. And I realized I had elevated art over everything else. My wife. My kids. Even Him. Art had become my god. My images became idols." Chuckling, "Talk about Old Testament tropes, right?... But my art became who I am instead of what I do. I've always known that what I can do is a gift. But I'd made the gift more important than the giver."

After a swallow of bourbon, Eve said, "I'm fascinated by people like you who talk to God that way. Have two-way conversations. I was raised Catholic. My grandparents took me to church. I did the whole first communion and confirmation thing. But I can't say I've ever really believed. I'm holding a grudge against God."

"Tell me why."

"For starters, he took my parents from me."

"How?"

"They died in a plane crash when I was three."

"I'm so sorry, Eve."

"Don't get me wrong, I had a very love-filled childhood. My grandparents were and still are absolutely incredible. I've been very fortunate. But there's still a hole."

"Of course. Especially as you got older and became more aware."

"But that's only the beginning of my grudge. There's everything I saw and did in Afghanistan. From watching the fear and panic grow and then the life drain from so many of my comrades' eyes as they gasped their last breath. To encountering a woman in Kabul whose wails of anguish still wake me at night."

"What happened?"

"Her husband was killed by a landmine. And she had just sold her newborn baby, a week old, to a stranger for a couple hundred dollars so she could feed her four other children."

"Oh, my word. That's horrible, Eve."

"It was. And let's not forget why I'm here… the Greater Boston Massacre. More than a half million people snuffed out in minutes. So, let's just say that God and I are not on the same speaking terms that you are."

"But you can be."

"Not interested. It's too late for me, anyway. Besides, there's much too much blood on my hands."

"It's never too late. God has plans and a purpose for every one of us. He redeems lost time. Restores us completely. Spiritually, mentally, emotionally, and I've seen him heal people physically. He can return us to factory settings, you might say. And I doubt you have more blood on your hands than King David. Many believe he slayed at least 80,000 men, probably more. And in spite of that, do you know what God said about him?"

"What?"

"David is a man after my own heart. That's where God looks. At our hearts."

"Mine's pretty dark, Brice. But I do admire and respect your beliefs. And your wisdom. But it's getting late." She stood up. "I should get some sleep. My flight to DC leaves at 6:00 a.m., so I'll need to leave here before 4:00 to get to Logan. I always enjoy talking to you, Brice."

"Thanks, Eve. I enjoy our times together, too. But I'm not sure if it's wisdom or just old age. None of us get to grow old without becoming familiar with grief and loss. And their offspring, regret."

"I may not be as old, but I am more than intimately familiar with all of those. In spades. Times a thousand. And I'd like to talk some more."

"Anytime, Eve."

"Are you a man of prayer?"

"I am."

"Please pray for me."

"Already have been."

As they headed toward the house, "Thank you for everything, Brice." She gave him a big hug. "It looks like Elise has gone to bed, so please thank her again for me. I'll be leaving so early tomorrow I won't see her."

"You've got my number. Don't be a stranger. Will I see you in December?"

"December?"

"Charlene's group exhibit at the Newbury. First show at the gallery in over a year and a half. Since the fire."

"Yes, of course! I did get her email. Completely forgot. I was working on a painting just before the attack. I hope to be back in Boston in the near future. I'll finish it for the show. Love a deadline."

"So, you're not painting in DC?"

"Not really. I have a sketchbook and some tubes of watercolor I work with occasionally. But I'm too busy trying to find out who else was behind the Massacre."

"Really. I didn't know."

"Please keep that to yourself, Brice."

"You have my word. And I'll pray even harder."

"Thank you. I need it. And it'll be nice to see you and everyone else in December. We could all use a bit of normalcy after an atrocious year."

They walked into the kitchen. As Brice placed their glasses

into the dishwasher, he said, "Looking forward to it."

"Thank you, Brice. For your hospitality. Your encouragement. For listening. It's been very long and very dark season."

Brice went to the kitchen island and picked up a small box and handed it to Eve. "For you."

"What's this?"

"Some light for your dark season. It's a Bible. I wasn't sure if you had one or not. And I've written a short inscription. May you also find the help and hope that I've found in its pages, Eve."

She placed it on the counter as she stepped over and hugged him again. "Thank you, Brice."

"My pleasure. You're not alone on this journey, Eve. And like all seasons, the dark one you've been in will change."

"I hope so."

"It will. You'll see."

Chapter 5

Eve—dressed in black Athleta leggings, her favorite pair because they had pockets on the hips and thighs, a long-sleeve, blue tee-shirt with a University of Toronto logo across the front, and dark-gray Nike running shoes—went out the front door of the Woodward Building, the Washington DC apartment complex she'd been living in for the past five months. She used one of the 30-foot tall ionic-style columns of polished marble that graced the front of the massive building's entrance to stretch her quads, hamstrings, and back before she pulled her sleeves up to her elbows and started running.

She went north on 15th Street at a casual pace. When she reached the corner of H Street in four hundred feet, she took a left and headed west. In another three hundred feet ran past the Dolly Madison House, across Madison Place and entered Lafayette Square at its northeast corner, past the statue of General Tadeusz Kościuszko.

She loved this historic park, a national landmark built in the 1820s by the renowned Boston architect, Charles Bulfinch, situated a mere hundred feet from the White House's north lawn. She had become intimately familiar with the paths that connected each of its four corners, all leading to a center oval. The arched brick pathways made their way through mature trees of nearly every American variety among well-manicured shrubs and bushes, some now in full bloom, past majestic statues of several iconic Revolutionary War heroes, like the Polish military engineer she had just breezed by.

As she rounded the statue of General Andrew Jackson, located in the center of the park, she recalled the story President Olson told her about Jackson. It was a couple of months ago at one of their clandestine meetings. She was heading to another one now.

At the slightest prompting, President Olson loved regaling those around him with lesser-known tidbits of American history, especially Revolutionary War history. It was something he had always done, long before he became President. Much to the chagrin of his wife and kids, and now to the bemusement of his staff and cabinet.

When America's seventh President was only14 years-old, he and his brother were captured by the British, who had abruptly shown up to occupy the home of a relative where the young Jacksons were staying. When a British officer demanded that Andrew polish his boots, he refused and in return for his obstinance this officer slashed him with his sword, leaving the young Jackson with scars on his left hand and head. Eve admired his fully formed feistiness and fortitude at such a young age. And she was certain that General Jackson would have been a formidable Special Forces commander if he were alive today.

She then ran down the path that curved toward the southwest corner of the park and exited at the Rochambeau statue, the French lieutenant general whose seven thousand troops joined up with Washington and Lafayette in the battles of Yorktown and the Chesapeake, victories that led to Lord Cornwallis' eventual surrender.

The whole trip took all of four minutes, nine when she

walked. She stopped running, went between some cars parked on Jackson Place, crossed the street and up the half-dozen stone stairs at number 716, a brick brownstone painted light beige. It was also known as the Presidential Townhouse.

716 Jackson Place was purchased by the U.S. Government in the late 50s and since the 60s has been used exclusively by former Presidents whenever they're in town. The four-story building, which contains two dining rooms, multiple bedrooms and a suite for a Secret Service detail in the basement, was comfortably refurbished by President George W. Bush during his first term in the early 2000s.

As soon as she got to the door, it was opened by a Secret Service agent, who said, "Hey, Eve. Right on time, as always."

"Nice to see you, Steven," Eve said, as he closed the door behind her. "How's the new baby?"

"She's great. Starting to sleep through the night, so that's a huge relief."

"Got a recent picture?"

"You bet," as he eagerly pulled out his cell, swiped a couple of times and held it up to Eve.

"Wow. She's gorgeous. She's gonna break some hearts. No doubt."

Smiling from ear to ear, "Thanks, Eve. The President's on his way, so you can head right down."

"Perfect. Thanks!" She made her way through the high-ceilinged, marble-floored hallway with its mural-painted walls. About halfway down, took a right at a small alcove with a tall, heavy oak door to the basement.

In the basement Secret Service suite, the living room contains a heavily reinforced steel door that opens to an underground tunnel connecting this building to the White House, a mere

700 feet to the southeast.

The tunnel door was hidden behind a large oak bookshelf that was hinged to swing away. Edward Stanton, another member of the President's Secret Service detail, was at the bookshelf as Eve entered the room.

They exchanged nods as she stood on the other side of the room, next to the white sofa with four square, blue pillows, each embroidered with the Presidential Seal, and watched as he pulled the bookshelf and swung it to the right, punched a five-digit code into the steel door's keypad and opened it.

Every time she watched this, Eve couldn't help feeling like she was in a scene from the movie *Clue.* Or the opening credits for the television show *Get Smart* that she and her college roommate would watch on MeTV, one of several old shows from the 60s they loved to binge watch and spoof. She thought, *Does this actually go to the White House, or to the billiard room? With the candlestick.*

Moments later, Jim Benton, head of the President's Secret Service detail entered from the tunnel, followed by the President, with agent Bill Brahms taking up the rear, who then closed the steel door as Edward swung the bookshelf back in place.

Or does it lead into the mind of John Malkovich?

"Good morning, Eve," said President Olson as he went to the sofa and motioned for Eve to sit next to him.

"Good morning, Mr. President."

The three Secret Service agents knew the drill and immediately headed down the hallway to the kitchen. Eve could hear and smell the brewing coffee.

Perhaps it's the entrance to the Batcave. Kapow!

Noticing her tee-shirt, "I didn't know you went to the University of Tears. I'm sure I read it somewhere in your file but forgot."

"Ah, so you know U of Toronto's reputation."

"I do. One of my nieces applied and got rejected. Tough school. Right up there with Harvard and the like. Birthplace of insulin, the first pacemaker, first electron microscope. A very impressive institution."

"You've done your homework, no pun intended."

"When Katie didn't get in, I was curious and did some digging. Excelling there says a lot about you."

"Appreciate it, Mr. President. But we're also Canadian. While the academic rigor can be brutal, we're nice and tend to help each other get through it."

Chuckling, "So I take it your major was art, yes?"

"Actually, art was my minor, sir. Cognitive Science was my major. I focused on art when I attended the Pennsylvania Academy of Fine Arts after graduating U of T."

"No kidding. What drew you to Cog Sci?"

"I fell in love with the wide range of disciplines it draws on. Understanding perception, language and reasoning. What it means to be conscious. Drawing on computer science, linguistics, human biology, philosophy and psychology. Mostly, I was attracted to learning to question not only what and how we think, but what thinking is."

"Skills, that've served you well. Clearly. And I bet all of that must feed into your art, too."

"Indeed, sir, it does."

"Okay. Well, let's get down to it, shall we. How was Boston?"

"Revelatory, sir. But first, let me say that your letter the priest read at Bonnato's memorial was very moving, Mr. President."

"Thanks, Eve. Some of that I owe to you. What you've told me about him. I'm also giving serious thought to a Medal of

Honor."

"That would…" She choked up for a moment. "That'd be very fitting, sir." After a beat. "So, the search of Hunter's apartment was more fruitful than I had hoped. We found his burner phone." She pulled an envelope from her pocket and handed it to him, "And we found this. I'm pretty sure it's how the cabal leader notifies other members when to turn on their burners. I had Boston PD forensics go over the envelope and letter, but only Hunter's prints were on them."

"Why do you think it's the leader?"

"When we analyzed all the communications between the Trahisons, we saw that they would use their normal cell phones to text very simple messages to each other. Like, 'Let's talk soon.' These synched up perfectly to the burner messages and conversations we wiretapped. Made sense. There was a natural relationship there. But that wouldn't likely be the case with anyone else in the cabal.

Eve continued. "Because the phones remained off and the batteries removed, they would need a way to innocuously convey a day and time to communicate. Email and messaging apps are too exposed and leave a trail. Much too risky. But postal mail coming from a lawn care company would be inconspicuous."

"Smart. No one'd look twice," the President replied.

"Except if you live in an urban apartment building. And hold onto a couple. I saw what looked like one or two others in Hunter's shredder. Glad he didn't get to these."

Placing the envelope onto the coffee table the President added, "Good break for us. So how do we leverage it?"

"I have something in mind. Heading to Langley tomorrow. Bringing the burner to a tech I trust. And while there, I'll take advantage of some of the most secure computers on the planet."

He stood. "Perfect. Think you'll have something in three days?"

"Yes, sir. I should," she said as she also stood.

"Good. Let's meet here then. Same Bat-time, same Bat-station."

So, Batcave it is. Thwack! Wham!

"Yes, Mr. President."

"I'm ready, Jim," the President called out toward the kitchen.

As the agents went about opening the bookshelf and metal door, Jim Benton spoke into his sleeve, "Wildcat is on the move."

After they left and Stanton, the agent who opened the door and was now closing the bookshelf back into place, Eve asked, "Hey, Ed, why is the President's code name, Wildcat? I've always wondered how you guys come up with these names."

"Each President is presented with a list, and they pick one. Could be an existing nickname, an area of expertise, an interest, a hobby, an alma mater, which is President Olson's. He's a Northwestern University alum. The Wildcats."

"Huh." Pointing to her shirt. "We're the Blue. Doesn't quite work."

"Actually, it could. Or perhaps, Joni."

"Joni?"

"Joni Mitchell. Her album, *Blue.*"

"Ah. So clever. If this Secret Service thing doesn't pan out, you may have a career in advertising."

Smiling, "But I'm already a mad man. And I hear advertising's such a brutal business I may actually be safer catching bullets for the president."

Chapter 6

Supreme Court Chief Justice Douglas Harrison was sitting at his desk in his chambers. He was going over the draft of a brief that his clerks, who would arrive in another hour, handed him yesterday. Missouri's attorney general had recently come to the high court with the unusual emergency request to sue New York.

Justice Harrison and a majority of his colleagues had recently handed down a ruling determining that former presidents cannot face criminal liability for their official acts, which greatly benefited former President Ronald Atout.

Now Missouri wanted to remove a gag order that New York had imposed on the former president when he was found guilty of fraud in that state. Citing this recent immunity ruling, attorney general Andrew Bagley wanted the gag order stayed until after the upcoming election.

Bagley stated that it limits what the former president, and now the GOP's confirmed presidential nominee, can say on the campaign trail. And that Atout's upcoming sentence could affect his ability to travel. *Yeah,* he thought, *jail cells do tend to limit travel to eight feet!*

It was a long shot. A legal Hail Mary, and Bagley knew it. And the Justice, along with his colleagues, was denying it.

But Harrison was having trouble concentrating and found

himself reading the same sentence for the third time. He kept looking at the cell phone on his desk. His *special* phone. The one no one saw. Or knew he had. The one he removed from the locked safe in his home office this morning. The one that had been quiet for the past three months. In fact, the last time it rang was during deliberations with his colleagues on said immunity ruling.

But he had received the notice in the mail two days ago. It told him when to have it turned on. So, he inserted the battery and powered it up fifteen minutes ago. What was distracting him wasn't so much that it would ring again shortly, or that the conversation would likely revolve around the Court's upcoming decisions and docket. He was thinking about the first time this phone rang, just over a year ago.

The caller had told him the Hamilton Brief was dead. And that all billable hours must stop. It was code for the completion of what became known as the Greater Boston Massacre. And this person mentioned that Senator Steven Trahison's legal services were just terminated. The not-so-thinly veiled implication being the caller was responsible for his death. And at the time the caller was completely confident that the senator's bill, H.R.7174, would still become law even without Trahison shepherding it through the Senate.

Which would mean complete control over every state's federal funds would be firmly placed into the hands of an Inspector General, a puppet oversight role the bill would have established.

That a parallel government, at least in terms of control over federal funds, would have been put in place right under the noses of the entire country.

That with this law the secret cabal that he and others were part of would be able to choke the unpredictable, left-leaning, self-righteous Blue states, especially those on each coast—the states that are the source of liberal, socialist poison currently infecting the country. And they would have had the power to enhance the impact and influence of the conservative Red states—influence the cabal believed they so rightly deserved as they took on the Great Satan, the godless left, in the eternal battle for America's soul.

The caller had said that the Senate's passage of H.R. 7174 and the president's signature was practically guaranteed.

The caller was wrong.

No one foresaw someone from the CIA and her Homeland team catching wind of their plot so quickly and intervening before the last phase of the plan could be executed, where DC would have suffered a more potently lethal fate than Boston had.

They had no clue that Eve Tuant would be their undoing.

And the cabal nearly ended.

But this work was far too important to abandon. The mission had become their North Star, their life's blueprint. For the justice, saving the nation from itself was just as important as being on the Supreme Court. It was why he was on the Bench. He was chosen to serve for such a time as this. And he knew it was the same for this caller.

So, they pivoted.

They would now use the courts to wield control and influence over the states. And former President Atout had handed them the ideal opportunity. Not only did he appoint Harrison as Chief, but he also managed to appoint two other conservative justices to the Court. They now held a 6-to-3 majority.

Both considered the former president to be a complete, incompetent fool. An embarrassing buffoon. But his many law-breaking, seditious missteps had also unintentionally set the stage for shifting the balance of power to their advantage.

As one of the Chief Justice's colleagues wrote in her dissenting remarks in the immunity ruling, "in every use of official power, the president is now a king above the law." And another wrote, "the Court today transfers from the political branches to itself the power to decide when the president can be held accountable."

They quickly recognized the opportunity this presented. They were looking well beyond the former president's circumstances, whose fate was inconsequential. His second term highly unlikely. The fact that he was nominated as his party's choice to run, given his exceedingly poor first-term performance four years ago, was a surprise and a gift.

They were handed a chance to write a Constitutional ruling for the future—their future, one that greatly enhanced the Executive and Judicial Branch's power, while at the same time doing an end-run around Congress and snubbing the people's will.

Making use of this jacked judicial power to accomplish their objectives was already in play.

Leveraging the newly attained power of presidential supremacy will be phase two.

When all looked irreversibly lost, this second chance was handed to them on a tainted silver platter. And they learned to never look a gift buffoon in the mouth.

The phone rang.

"Hello?"

"Good morning, Your Honor."

"Good morning."

"I know your clerks will be arriving soon, so I'll keep this short. Where do things stand with Chevron?" She was referring to the landmark 1984 decision stating that the federal courts should generally defer to a government agency's reasonable interpretation of an ambiguous regulatory law. That these agencies, who are experts in their fields, know the intricate and often highly technical details better than the judges in these cases.

But thanks to Harrison the court agreed to take up a case involving the same question, and now the high court was poised to abolish the Chevron doctrine. If so, the federal courts alone would now determine the meaning of regulatory law. Technical and scientific expertise be damned. Disparaged. And disregarded.

It was a judicial power grab, plain and simple. With more to come.

He replied, "I'm fairly certain it will be another six-to-three decision in our favor. The opinion that I'm currently drafting will state that federal law governing administrative agencies, as well as federal courts' review of agency actions, will now require the courts to decide legal questions by applying their own judgment. The doctrine of deference established by the Chevron ruling will no longer apply."

"Excellent news, Douglas! Well done. One more plank in our platform. Rung on our ladder."

"Thank you… Something else I've been pondering. How will the immunity decision play out if Atout wins the next election? I know it's unlikely, especially after his recent horrendous debate performance. President Olson ate his lunch. Stole his lunch money. And gave him a black eye to boot. I've never seen a former president so unintelligent, so thin-skinned and so easily baited. But since he seems to still have such a large number of citizens under his cultish spell, we must ask, what if?"

"He won't win. Olson will get his second term. Then we make our next move."

Harrison said, "Providing the Senate doesn't get its way

with legislation to reverse our immunity ruling. The No Kings Act is gaining traction. Certainly among Democrats. Some Republicans, too."

"Unlikely to get anywhere in our landlocked Congress." Chuckling, "But we'll blow up that bridge when we come to it."

He visibly winced. He thought her comment cut a little too close. It was too soon. The more than half million innocent citizens killed in the Massacre were still fresh in the country's collective minds. And in his.

But all he said was, "Got it."

She added, "I'm in awe of the fact that Chevron is about to end. That thanks to you, forty years of precedent will become fair game. We can now take advantage of this ruling's profound destabilization. Leverage the fact that that even the most well-settled agency regulations can now be placed on the chopping block. And that will enable us to use the courts to subtly choke the Blue states by targeting those regulations that most impact them. Mr. Justice, you are a genius."

"Appreciate the kudos. But, once again, our former president unknowingly got us here. If he didn't appoint me as Chief and the other two justices that he did, we wouldn't have the six-to-three majority needed to make all this possible."

She replied, "I only wish all presidents were as easy to manipulate as he was. Still is. A little flattery and ego stroking from the right people and he melts like butter."

"Now we'll use that butter to fry our enemies." As the words left his mouth, he recoiled internally, realizing he had just done what she did. Up to this point, he had felt superior to her. Believed he was above her. Better. She was a politician; he was a Supreme Court justice. Chief Justice, in fact. His job was for life. Hers was eight years, at best. But the realization that they were perhaps more alike than he thought jarred him. While he never actually killed anyone, he was complicit in the senator's death and mass murder. Thoughts he had been somewhat successful in suppressing up to this point. He suspected that this was the reason he had been having so much trouble sleeping these past several months.

"Indeed. You are shaping history, Mr. Justice," she replied.

"*We* are shaping history, Ma'am."

"Yes, we are… I'll reach out in a couple weeks. Usual method. We'll talk next steps."

"Until then." And the line went dead.

Chapter 7

It took Eve forty-five minutes to drive from her apartment on 15th Street to CIA headquarters in Langley. She had just exited Route 123, also known as Dolly Madison Boulevard, and was making her way down Colonial Farm Road to enter the CIA campus at the southwest gate.

As she considered her daily run past Dolly Madison's house and her frequent drives on this road that also bears her name, it struck Eve that what our fourth President's wife was so well known for—holding social functions where she invited members of both political parties, introducing the practice of bipartisan cooperation—that Congress needed to Dolly Madisonize itself once again.

That today's Senate and House had greatly regressed and devolved. Congress once again closely resembled the Jeffersonian politics of Dolly's time, where the meeting of both political parties often became violent affairs with frequent physical altercations and occasional duels.

Madison had pioneered and fostered the notion that members of each party could amicably socialize, network, and negotiate with each other without violence.

Eve thought, *Congress needs more Dollys, fewer dicks.*

After showing the guard her ID and finding a spot to park in the smaller western lot near the water tower, she made her way to the walkway leading to the main front door of the original headquarters building, where the iconic CIA seal is embedded in the marble floor and the Memorial Wall of nameless stars is in the foyer—each one representing a fallen CIA operative.

The sun was intense in the cloudless sky, and she could smell the potent jasmine-like scent of the hydrangeas blooming next to her as her shadow walked across them. A hundred feet from the main door, she took a left at the intersecting walkway that led north and entered another building on the northwest corner.

She had her ID badge hanging from a lanyard on her neck and showed it to the guard. It contained nothing more than her picture and a bar code—the CIA never being one to advertise who worked for them. Eve stood in front of the iris and facial recognition scanner as the guard watched his screen.

After a moment the guard said, "Nice to see you again, Ms. Tuant."

As she walked past him, she said, "I told you, Eliot, call me Eve."

"Yes, Ma'am."

Smiling, "And definitely not Ma'am."

"Yes, Ms. Tuant… Eve. Know your way, Ma— Eve?"

"Like the back of my hand."

After taking an elevator down three levels, she headed left at a long hallway of identical oak doors and stopped at one of them on the right, knocked as she entered. "Hello, it's me. Leo, you in?"

A voice from the far corner behind a cubical wall said, "Back here, Eve."

"Hiding?" she asked.

"While hiding in plain sight is pretty much the stock-in-trade of this building, I'm actually tweaking a new texting encryption app I'm working on. Almost done. Just added some AI code. This thing will be unbreachable. As soon as you activate it, it disables your phone's camera, mic, and GPS. And a kill switch deletes the data. Like it never existed."

"Didn't the Dutch crack something like this several years ago? Called Sky something?"

"They did. With the Belgians. And behind the scenes, I helped break the algorithm."

"Did you? Why am I not surprised."

"Sky ECC. Became popular with the underworld. This one won't be available. And if anyone nefarious does get a hold of it, I can kill switch it, anywhere in the world. From here. And it can't be breached. My secret sauce is in the artificial intelligence."

Leo Burns looked nothing like a tech geek. At least not like the typical caricature Hollywood tended to serve up. While he did wear glasses, even sitting at a monitor couldn't hide his six-foot-three, 230-pound frame of ropy muscle which, when added to an off-the-charts IQ, serves him well as a CIA officer. And it also served him well in Afghanistan as a Special Operations Command (SOC) Marine. Brawn and brains, a double threat the Taliban felt in spades.

He had served under Eve's command for three years. Eve's Afghanistan team consisted of six Canadian JTF2 members, three U.S. SOC Marines, of which Leo was one, and three Green Berets. The fact that these twelve, highly skilled, very independent, territorial, and extremely lethal warriors operated as a seamless team spoke directly to Eve's leadership skills.

And Leo and Eve had remained close friends ever since. Few bonds are tighter than friendships forged in combat. It's a connection of souls. A trust that transcends nearly all others. You become part of each other. Like the bond of marriage but formed in a different way—through shared hardships, pain, trauma, intense fear, dark humor, and pure adrenaline. It's unbreakable. And lifelong. Often lasting even beyond this life—as many of those who survive often care for the graves and families of their fallen brethren.

It was Eve who recommended Leo to the CIA brass when their tour of Afghanistan ended. And he's been happy as a pig in poop, his words, ever since.

She said, "I prefer organic intelligence over artificial. Costs a bit more, but worth it."

"Funny. You should do standup."

"But I am. My audience just happens to be one at a time. I'll be here all week. Tip your waitress."

Waving his right hand back and forth at the wrist. "Listen to the sound of my one-handed applause… Whatcha got for me?"

She handed him Hunter's burner and its battery. "This. Need everything on it."

"The traitor's phone?"

"Yup."

"Then the numbers and messages will likely be those of other burners, correct?"

"Uh, huh. And I know where you're going. Will folks at these numbers still have them? There's been no mention in public or in our internal reports about burners being used by the Massacre conspirators. That omission was very intentional. You're one of only seven others who knows these even exist."

"Got it. Only been a year since they were used, so it's quite possible they're still in play. Hopefully. Give me a couple hours to make it give up all its secrets."

"And tell no one else, right? No other Agency colleagues. Or bosses. Even if they ask?"

"On my life."

"Thanks, Leo. Meanwhile, point me to a computer I can use to run something else down."

"Use this one over here," he said as he stood, towering over Eve by nearly a foot in height and width, stepped into an adjoining cubical and powered up the monitor on the desk. "All yours."

"Perfect. Thanks!"

After logging on, Eve opened a secure browser and went to the U.S. Postal Service website. After a few clicks she was looking at the Postal Service's Informed Delivery pages. This service provides a daily email to those who sign up with a preview that includes a photo of the postal mail about to arrive in their mailbox.

The executive assistants and secretaries of most members of Congress and many of the federal judges, including the Supreme Court justices, used this service to help them manage the often-overwhelming volume of snail mail that still comes their way every day.

Using Overlord, the CIA's program that can get into any computer anywhere in the world without being detected or leaving a trace, Eve was able to look at these pages for each senator. She typed in some search prompts to locate any mail that may have come from Earthworks Lawn Care over the past six months for every one of the one hundred senators. After an hour of searching, the program came up empty. She then went back another six months. Still nothing.

She then did the same for each of the nine Supreme Court justices and struck pay-dirt within minutes. Only one justice had received any mail from Earthworks. Justice Douglas Harrison. The Chief Justice had received three Earthworks mailings over the last eight months. The most recent was just four days ago.

"Holy shit!" she said more loudly than she meant to.

"Is that a good holy shit or a bad holy shit?" Leo asked from across the room.

Eve went over and sat in the chair next to his desk and told him the whole story. What she had just now discovered. Everything that had happened in the year leading up to the Greater Boston Massacre. The reason she was now working in DC. And what she'd been doing ever since she arrived.

She had been considering doing this for two days. She wanted another ally in DC. Someone besides the president and Alex Marshall, the President's Secretary of Homeland Security. Someone who, if needed, could be boots on the ground with her. And she didn't think it was necessary to ask the president. Felt it was her call. Like in-the-moment decisions she had to make on the battlefield. But she would certainly let the president know that Leo was now on the team. And she had decided she would ask President Olson to meet with her tomorrow.

So, she told Leo what the media had left out of the Massacre coverage and reports, which was everything about her relationship with Hunter. Everything that happened in the lighthouse. About the cabal's other members—another senator, a Supreme Court justice, who, with Eve's discovery, they now knew to be the Chief Justice, and a yet-to-be-identified person known only as *someone in the President's inner circle.*

And she told him that she had been reporting directly to the president and secretly meeting with him regularly.

When she was done, Leo said, "Holy shit."

Smiling, Eve said, "Is that a good holy shit or a bad one? So that's why I'm actually surprised no one else in the Senate got one of these mailers. And I went back an entire year. Nada."

"Did someone get it wrong? Was it a senator or perhaps a

member of the House?"

"*Senator* was stated. But I suppose it's a possible mistake and it's a Representative instead. Shit. That's 435 names to look at."

Leo continued, "Either way, with Justice Harrison's leadership, these folks have obviously shifted from trying to pass a law to using the courts to reach their end goal, which appears to be to suppress liberal states and support conservative ones by using the judicial branch, in partnership with the executive branch.

"Not only does it appear they've pivoted away from creating new legislation to achieve that goal, they're also doing an end-run around the legislative branch entirely.

"Look at the Supreme Court's most recent rulings. They've dissolved long-standing legal precedents, some five and six decades old. It gives the courts themselves more power. More dominance. And they've clearly favored the former president, the Chief Felon, the Commander in Thief, President Felonious Monk."

"My, my, tell us how you really feel."

"Like most of the country, I once held the Supreme Court in the highest regard. To me they were untouchable icons of justice and veracity. They were revered. Stalwart. Resolute. There was an aura about them. Almost otherworldly. But no longer. Some have been taking huge sums of money in the form of trips, college tuitions, vacations and who knows what other gratuities from business leaders with a political and legal axe to grind. Some with stakes in upcoming Supreme Court cases. It's shameful. These are supposed to be people above reproach. Held to a higher standard. Steering clear of anything with even hints of a conflict of interest. But that's all down the toilet.

"And their recent immunity ruling completely shattered the bedrock foundation this country was built on—that no one is above the law. Now apparently one person is. The Dishonorable

Delinquent. The King of Pain."

"And the hits keep on coming."

"I'm pissed. It's like Lady Justice is no longer blind. She has lifted her blindfold, uncovered her right eye and is now staring directly at a future constitutional crisis of her own making."

After a beat he said, "There may be another reason you didn't see any senators getting these mailers. It could also answer the question of who the unknown cabal member from the President's inner circle may be. What if it's the Vice President?"

"Why her?"

"What's the one Executive Branch member who is also a member of the Senate?"

"Fuck… the VP."

"Yup. Her other title is President of the Senate. Votes when there's a tie."

"Shit! If true, this is huge, Leo. You may have busted this thing wide open, and you haven't even finished with the phone yet."

"Yes, I have." Handing her a six-page printout with numbers and text messages.

"Wow. That was quick. Whatever the Agency is paying you it's not enough."

"They pay me plenty. Honestly, I love this work so much I'd do it for free. Just don't tell my boss I said that. And I wouldn't be here if not for you, Eve."

"Oh, I'm not so sure about that, Leo. Talent like yours would have gotten their attention eventually."

"Maybe. But you made it happen. And I'll never forget it."

"Nor will I ever forget how many times you saved my ass when shit went sideways in 'Stan."

"We saved each other's asses. The whole team." Smiling, "And if I do say so, it's a nice ass. Well worth saving."

She smiled back and lightly punched his arm as she stood and returned to her cubicle to shut down the computer, grabbed her things and said, "So, are you in?"

"You knew I'd be in when you told me all of this."

"Just tickin' the box."

"I'm in. Both feet."

"Then can you do me another favor?"

"Name it."

Looking at the pages. "Here are the texts that Hunter sent Trevor, Senator Trahison's Chief of Staff." Pointing at them, "So we can eliminate these two numbers. That leaves these other three. Is it possible to monitor them?"

"Yup. Can monitor all of 'em. Only take about an hour to set them up. I'll get a notification when any of them are in use."

"That's awesome, Leo. I'll probably reach out to the person who helped me wiretap Senator Trahison's phone last year and have him do the same for Justice Harrison's office, cell, and home phones. If one of these numbers is his burner, your notification will verify it."

Leo said, "I'll do you one better. I'll put the taps in place. I can do it from here. No need to bring anyone else into this. I can also turn on the justice's cell phone mic. If his phone's nearby when he's on a burner, whether it's one of these numbers or another, we'll hear everything he says. And I'll record it. After that, I'll be able to tap whichever burner is his. If the other burners are activated once my monitor's in place, I'll then wiretap those as well. And once we've identified who the burner phones belong to, I'll tap their regular phones, too. I've got an algorithm set up that will record and transcribe any calls or texts and store them here."

"Holy shit! And that's a good holy shit, by the way. Harrison won't know?"

"Not a clue. Can also turn on his cell's camera if you want. The only very minor inconvenience is that I need to physically be here to access and download the transcriptions. Or I can connect from my laptop at home on the CIA's direct VPN. Don't want this stuff in the Cloud, even a secure one."

"Wow. Glad I'm on your side."

"We gonna wiretap the V.P., too?"

"Not yet. Let's see if she's the person the justice talks to. If so, we'll see what the president wants to do.

"Got it."

Eve added, "I've created access to Harrison's Informed Delivery account. So, I'll let you know as soon as I see the next Earthworks mailer. Probably gives us a two- or three-day window."

"Before you go, give me your cell and I'll put my encryption app on it. We can exchange texts with absolute security. Use it to let me know when the justice gets his mail. But more importantly, I want you to use it if things heat up for you in any way, Eve. These fuckers have already proven how dangerous they are. Wherever, whenever. You need me, I'm there. In a heartbeat."

"Thanks, Leo," she said as she handed her phone to him. "That goes both ways, you know."

"I know. You'll cover my ass, too."

"Yup. And if I do say so, it's a nice ass. Well worth covering."

Chapter 8

Robin Spinner had just returned to her West Wing office from the Senate floor, where her vote broke the 50-to-50 tie to nominate Margaret Gilbert to be a United States District Judge for Massachusetts. Justice Gilbert will now serve on one of the 62 district courts in that state, thanks to Vice President Spinner.

Most of her tie-breaking votes over the last two years have been for judicial appointments that President Olson had been making. Given that his predecessor had packed the Supreme Court with staunch, right-leaning conservative Republicans, Olson was highly motivated to create some judicial balance by filling vacant lower court judgeships with as many Democrats as possible before the next election.

Not that party affiliation really mattered much in interpreting the law. It was more about ideological worldview. More about the lens through which a judge perceived the world. While a broad generalization, judges who were Democrats tended to skew with more favor to the underdog, have more sympathy for the weaker party in a case.

In President Olson's thinking, the need for lower court judges with an eye for the underdog in ideologically controversial issues, such as affirmative action, capital punishment, and sex discrimination should help counterbalance what he viewed as right-wing odium.

In light of the appointment of three conservative justices that had occurred in the Supreme Court during his predecessor's administration, it was a small comfort. But he'll take what he can get.

In a Senate that was split right down the partisan middle, Robin Spinner had now shattered the record for most tie-breaking votes made by any vice president in the nation's 250-year history.

But almost every vote she made in the Democrats' favor grated on her somewhat—took off a bit more skin. While clearly a Democrat in name and policy-making ideology during her entire political career as governor of Illinois, then Senator, and now V.P., Robin Spinner was actually a closet Constitutional originalist. Neither Democrat nor Republican. Actually, a Federalist, to put a label on it. While the Federalist party was the very first party to form in the United States, and came to an end sometime around 1825, it still lived on in her heart and soul.

Vice President Robin Spinner shared the late Senator Steven Trahison's admiration for Alexander Hamilton and his Federalist ideologies and writings. She longed, as the senator once did, for a greater degree of federal control over the unpredictable, mostly coastal Blue states and their dangerous liberal, socialist convictions.

While Illinois is also a prominent Blue state, Spinner had to be extremely subtle in how she shaped her state's legislation. The fact that she was called a moderate Democrat by her colleagues, the media, and political pundits spoke to how well she had learned to walk the Blue/Red line with a delicate balance.

It's why she had worked so hard to do whatever she had to do, including ordering the end of people's lives, to make certain that Senator Trahison's bill would become law and finally accomplish her deepest political and ideological longings.

Her insatiable Federalist hunger would have finally been sated.

But Eve Tuant had tipped over the dinner table.

When the decision was made to make Boston the target for the required 9/11-like event needed to trigger the control clause in Senator Trahison's bill, the vice president proposed that Hunter Forte join the Boston Homeland team and get close to Eve.

She did so because she knew something of Eve Tuant's reputation. She had read a Top-Secret report covering Tuant's extremely impressive counterintelligence work around the globe and more recently in Boston for the Marathon bombing. While she was aware of how formidable Eve could be, she was confident that her plan would not become perceptible until it was too late, if at all. And Hunter would be her eyes and ears.

That error in judgment became readily apparent as Eve began putting the pieces together. It all happened much quicker than the vice president, Senator Trahison or Hunter had anticipated. And when Eve had set out to confront the Senator, it forced Spinner's hand to end his life to preserve the cabal and its essential mission.

Truth be told, she also did it to save her own hide.

A threat of life in prison at the very least, and the even stronger likelihood of being executed for high treason and mass murder tended to trump ideology and morality.

But killing the senator ironically turned out to be one of the best decisions she's made in her long climb to nearly the top of the world's pinnacle of power. While she would have been happy to guide her Federalist strategies and tactics from behind the scenes, fate had thrust her front and center.

Now she was just a heartbeat away from the presidency, from being in the position to greatly affect the country's direction, to have a level of decision-making impact that she never considered possible only a year ago.

Now it was within her grasp.

And once she gets her hands on the wheel, the recent Supreme Court's immunity ruling means she can drive without guardrails. Or speed limits. *Woo-hoo, we're on a roll now!*

As things cooled down after the Greater Boston Massacre, it became evident that the rest of the cabal's secrets died with the senator. And the vice president wasn't at all upset that Hunter also met his demise at the lighthouse.

It saved her from finding another way to accomplish that same end.

When she believed it was safe to reconnect with the Chief Justice and discuss other ways to move forward, it didn't take his brilliant legal mind long to devise a strategy that would in essence achieve the cabal's main objective. Doing this through the judicial system, they knew, would simply take more time and be a bit more unpredictable.

But then, lo and behold, President Ronald Atout came onto the scene, and he set the stage for the Supreme Court to give their strategy an amphetamine shot in the ass. *Woo-hoo, we're on a roll now!*

Combining these recent judicial power expansions with a president willing to wield this new, unprecedented executive power meant gaining even more control over the states than Senator Trahison's law would have made possible. Now instead of just fiscal control, they were close to gaining control of both the judicial and executive branches. Control and influence of the purse strings would naturally follow suit.

As the country's president, Spinner could simply write decrees to fulfill her Federalist longings, circumvent the legislative branch, and ignore the people. Once the lawsuits began to challenge her decrees, thanks to the Chief Justice, the Supreme Court was already poised to tip decisions in her favor.

In Chief Justice Douglas Harrison, Spinner felt she had her own version of John Marshall, the Chief Justice whose three decades of Federalist principles, rulings, and decisions, from the early 1800s through the 1830s, shaped and confirmed the supremacy of the federal government and the federal Constitution over the states'.

Marshall had taken the mere 154 words the framers wrote in the Constitution's 6th Article and turned them into volumes of substantial, precedent-setting decisions.

The Vice President and Chief Justice were well on their way to once again reshaping the law of the land into a neoteric, Marshall-esque image for the next millennium.

But the specter of Eve Tuant was still haunting her.

Did Tuant learn more about the cabal than was reported in the media and national security reports she read? Did Hunter reveal anything he shouldn't have? Did either of the Trahisons? Was Eve still working behind the scenes to suss out the cabal and uncover her role or the justice's?

Her thoughts were interrupted by a rap on the door as it was being opened by Jean Fox, the VP's Chief of Staff, who said, "Welcome back, Madame Vice President. How'd it go?"

"Fine. Another judicial confirmation tiebreaker. Massachusetts this time."

"That makes 34, doesn't it?"

"Yup. And counting. Beginning to feel like we're playing basketball instead of rendering Senate confirmations. We broke the nation's record for most tie-breaking votes this year. Maybe Wilt Chamberlain's record is next."

"How many was that?"

"A hundred."

"Look out, Wilt the Stilt; Spinner's the winner."

Smiling. "Cute… So, what's next?"

"You've got a meeting with the president and some NSC members in twenty minutes."

"Right. Almost forgot. He called this smaller group of the National Security Council meeting last minute. Remind me what it's about?"

"An update on AUKUS."

"Right. Could you bring me the file with my notes from the last meeting?"

"Already on your desk."

"What would I do without you?"

"Oh, you'd do plenty. Just not as efficiently."

"You're worth your weight in gold, Jean."

"Now *that's* what I call one hell of an incentive to quit Ozempic."

Chapter 9

The AUKUS meeting in the Oval Office had been going on for about a half hour. On the two beige sofas that faced each other in front of the fireplace sat Secretary of State Michelle Rosen, Secretary of Defense Albert Barnes, Secretary of Homeland Security Alex Marshall, and General Thaddeus Wall, Chairman of the Joint Chiefs of Staff.

The president and vice president sat next to each other in the two chairs at the end of each sofa, their backs to the Resolute desk. And each of their chiefs of staff sat in chairs on the other ends of the sofas, in front of the fireplace.

The President asked, "So what's the latest with Canada?"

Michelle Rosen said, "They want in on Pillar 2, sir."

The AUKUS trilateral security partnership between Australia, the UK and the US was formed "to promote a free, open, secure and stable Indo-Pacific." This is what the public announcement stated. But its unspoken, not-so-thinly veiled purpose is to deter China from continuing to throw its considerable and growing military weight around in the region unchecked and unopposed. The partnership has two pillars. Pillar 1 provides Australia with nuclear-powered submarines. And Pillar 2 offers cooperative development, innovation, and information sharing in six technology areas: undersea capabilities, quantum technologies, artificial intelligence and autonomy, advanced cyber, hypersonic and counter-hypersonic capabilities, and electronic warfare.

The President said. "Took 'em long enough. Lafleur caught a lot of flak by his political opponents for being left out. His comeback was he wasn't interested in nuclear subs. But Pillar 2 is right up his alley."

"It's optics, sir. His rival during their election campaign said he'd join AUKUS if elected. The Prime Minister didn't want to appear reactionary."

Defense Secretary Barnes added, "Canada's looking forward to participating in quantum technologies, as well as advanced cyber, artificial intelligence and undersea tech platforms."

The President said, "Good. They'll be a great asset in those areas. Lots of intellectual horsepower in our neighbor to the north. Be nice to tap it. What about Japan?"

Barnes replied, "They're still hot to trot."

"So, what's the holdup?" the President asked.

"Australia and the UK, sir. They're extremely concerned by Japan's lack of security. They don't think they can adequately protect the highly sensitive information."

"Didn't Australia invite them to join, for crissake?"

"They did, Mr. President. But that was before their intelligence folks did some security assessments and before we got our own security report from the NSA. I think all parties assumed that Japan was as buttoned up as the rest of us. They are not. And we now share the Aussies' and Brits' concerns."

"So how do we fix it?"

General Wall said, "We're conducting a joint assessment with their military now, Mr. President. Coming at their broader security issues from that side of the house. Since their primary interest is in hypersonic weapons development and strengthening their electronics warfare platform, we can leverage that to get them to button up their entire security infrastructure. The Japanese are motivated, sir. I expect they'll be ready next year."

"Be nice to get them in sooner. Their role in keeping China in check is pinnacle. They could very well be the tip of the spear if shit hits the fan."

"Let me see what fires I can light, Mr. President," the General replied.

The President's secretary, Liz Clark, quietly came in and stood by the door after she closed it. She didn't do this while meetings were in progress unless it was something critical. He waved her over and she hurried to his side to whisper into his ear.

"Eve needs to see you as soon as possible, sir."

Given Robin Spinner's proximity to the President, even though Liz whispered, she overheard. Her eyes widened and her face froze for a moment on hearing the name. *Could it be her? The same Eve Tuant?* she thought.

Other than the president, no one else knew or used Eve's name. While Liz had never met Eve, she was told by the president to let him know anytime she called. Day or night. Any hour. No exceptions. And Eve was told if she needed him beyond their regular meetings, to reach out to Liz at a confidential White House extension number, and to only use her first name. This was only the second time a call from Eve had come in. Liz actually thought Eve was a codename.

The President nodded, looked at his watch and quietly replied, "Tell her an hour and a half."

Robin's mind was racing. *She's here in DC? Not Boston? And he's meeting with her? Why? Shit! This can't be good. Not at all. Damn it!*

She found it hard to pay attention to the rest of the meeting as the team went over a list of other countries in favor of the new alliance and had said so publicly, others who wish to take part, and the countries who are opposed to it, mainly China, Russia, North Korea and Iran. No surprise coming from the postmodern Axis of Evil.

They also covered China's threats to Australia after the AUKUS announcement. China's party-owned tabloid, *Global Times*, denounced Australia and said they had now turned themselves into an adversary of China. That China would punish them without mercy. And Australian troops will most likely be the first western soldiers to die in the South China Sea.

President Olson said, "Kinda stupid, don't ya think? They just told the world why it needs AUKUS and other alliances like it. But then the devil does tend to overplay his hand, doesn't he."

After the meeting ended, Robin did her best to break away and return to her office as quickly as she could. Jean Fox had noticed her boss' distraction as soon as Liz Clark left the Oval.

So did the president.

Chapter 10

Robin Spinner hurried down the West Wing hallway to her office with Jean barely able to keep up. As she strode through the outer office and got to her door, her face still taut, she said, "Please see that I'm not disturbed for the next hour, Jean. No calls. No visitors. No exceptions. Except for the president, of course."

"Is everything okay? Madame, Vice President… Robin, how can I help?" Jean asked, her concern evident in her voice and etched in her face.

"I'm fine. Leaving me alone is all the help I need right now," she said more tersely than she meant to as she swung her door closed.

She fumbled in her purse for her vape pen and took a long draw as she began to pace in front of her desk. She had quit smoking cigarettes and switched to this more discrete, less offensive nicotine delivery method after the election. She was very close to quitting completely. But if Eve Tuant was indeed in town, then she was going to need all the nerve-settling help she could get. She had to confirm three things: whether this was actually Eve Tuant. If so, was she was really in DC.? And lastly and most importantly, why was she here?

There was only one person she could task with finding out.

She went back into her purse and removed her burner phone

and inserted the battery. Fortunately for her, while their use was discouraged, personal cell phones were not monitored in the White House. But, because cell signals could be detected, when using her burner phone, she had to keep her calls and texts short. And coded.

She dialed and after one ring, "Hello?"

"Hi, Courtney, it's me. Just wanted to remind you to feed the cat. She eats at seven. Don't forget."

"I won't."

"Bye." She ended the call, powered off the phone, removed the battery and dropped both back into her purse.

Chapter 11

Eve had arrived at the Presidential Townhouse fifteen minutes earlier. She stood in front of the sofa as the president entered through the tunnel door and came over to Eve. Pointing to the coffee cups Eve had placed on the marble coffee table that ran much of the sofa's length, he said. "Is that what I think it is?"

"Yes, Mr. President. It's *Haiti Blue*. I heard it was your favorite. Zeke's Coffee is on my block, sir."

As he gestured for her to sit with him, he took one of the cups and said, "Best coffee on the planet." He took a sip. "Oooh, ya, that's the stuff."

"This is for you, too, Mr. President," as she handed him a brown paper bag of whole bean coffee, the black and white Zeke's Coffee logo on the front.

"Well, thank you, Eve! I think you've just earned a spot on the list of Medal of Freedom recipients."

Smiling, she said, "Had I known it was that easy I would have sent you an entire case a long time ago, sir."

After a short chuckle, he said, "I'm going to have the White House kitchen start stocking this. I don't know why I didn't do it earlier." After a beat added, "So why are we here, Eve?"

As she told him what she discovered about the Chief Justice

by searching the USPS Informed Delivery site, his brow knitted nearly into a knot. But when she told him about Leo and his theory of the vice president potentially being the hidden cabal member in his inner circle, his jaw dropped as he whispered, "Holy shit."

"A lot of that going around, Sir."

He then went silent for a long moment before adding, "This actually makes sense. Would explain her behavior this afternoon." He then told her what he noticed after his secretary informed him of Eve's meeting request. "She must have overheard Liz whisper your message to me. Could be why she was so rattled. And now she knows you're here in DC. Or strongly suspects it. We'll need absolute proof of her involvement."

Eve told him about the phone bugging plan and her set-up to access the justice's Informed Delivery account. "We'll know soon enough, Mr. President."

"So, tell me more about Leo."

"Think Einstein's brain in Schwarzenegger's body. See-though-walls brilliant. IQ somewhere north of 160. One of the best counterintelligence and combat strategists I've ever worked with. And I've never seen a better shooter. Any weapon. Watched him take out an elusive Taliban big-wig we'd been tracking for two months with a single TAC-50 shot from two miles away. There's no one I'd want more working with me in DC and no one I trust more, Mr. President."

"Two miles?" Shaking his head in awe, "Sounds like you're in good hands, Eve. And a good man to have on the team. It's none of my business and you don't have to answer, but are the two of you an item? Just wondering. The way you talk about him."

"God no. He's like a brother, Mr. President. Closer than a brother, actually. While we flirt, more like buddy banter, we'd never cross that line. Our relationship was forged in combat. It's hard to explain our connection, sir, unless you've been there."

"Got it. And I think I understand."

"Besides, he's been with his current girlfriend for a few years now. Which I admire. Vets like us tend to struggle with relationships."

"I've seen the stats. Why I've been pushing Congress for more VA mental health funding. Way too many vet suicides. We need to do something about it."

"And we appreciate it, Mr. President."

"We owe you and every vet a debt we can never truly repay. It's the least we can do. Back to Robin. If she's involved in this, either she and or the justice are probably behind Senator Trahison's demise. Could be both. Not sure if the justice is wired to order a hit on someone, but I think Robin could. She could actually be the one pulling all the cabal's strings. Who knows what she may do when it comes to you, Eve."

"I'm more concerned for you, Mr. President."

"I can keep her at arm's length. Do so in a way that doesn't arouse suspicion." He held his hands to each temple like a swami, "I believe I see some overseas trips in her future... Remind me of the name you're using here in DC."

"I'm renting my apartment under my great, great grandmother's maiden name, Rose Genest."

"Lovely name... Let's assume she'll start looking for you. Confirm you're here. An alias should at least slow her search a bit."

"The Agency did a full fake background for me." Pulling her wallet out of her small backpack and extracting her license. "See. Not an exact likeness, but close."

"Couldn't the CIA do a better job with that?"

"It's intentional, sir. Adds a little smoke to the mirror, so to speak.”

“Ah. Got it. Some cloak to your dagger.”

“Speaking of cloaks, Mr. President. Leo created and installed an unbreachable texting encryption app on our phones.” She removed a tablet from her backpack. “Leo put the install setup here, sir. With your permission, I’d like to add it to yours. The three of us will be able to communicate completely undetected. I won’t need to go through Liz again to reach you.”

As he handed her his cell phone and looked over his shoulder down the hall toward the kitchen where his Secret Service agents were sitting and talking, he nearly whispered, “Just us chickens, okay?”

“Absolutely... I’ve heard that expression several times. Definitely an American turn of phrase. But where does it come from?”

“An old joke. The 1900s, I think. A farmer surprises a chicken thief in the act. Stands outside the coop with his shotgun and says, ‘who’s in there.’ Thief says, ‘nobody here but us chickens.’”

“Cute.”

“Funny part is the farmer bought it.”

“Let’s hope that happens here, too.”

Chapter 12

Vice President Spinner was lost in thought as she sat in the back seat of her armored Dodge Durango, two of her Secret Service detail up front. Their car was followed by an armored Ford Explorer with the three remaining detail members.

Because she wasn't paying attention, the 2.5-mile trip from the White House to One Observatory Circle happened in a blink. As they took a left from Massachusetts Avenue and entered the first security gate to the US Naval Observatory property, where the official VP residence was located, she gathered her things onto her lap as they drove up Observatory Lane's hill and through the gate of the separate, highly secured and walled grounds that surrounded the house.

When the car stopped in front of the stately Queen Anne-style home that had been the official vice-presidential residence since 1974, Robin jumped out of the back seat and bound up the front stairs, across the broad wrap-around veranda and through the front door.

She made her way to the middle of the entryway and took the stairs to the second floor two at a time, briskly down the hallway, past the bedroom, past one of several fireplace inglenooks located throughout the 9,000-square foot home built in 1893 and still retained much of its 19th century charm, and entered her study.

After placing her briefcase and purse on top of the desk, she reached into her purse for her burner phone and inserted the battery. Noting that she had another fifteen minutes before her call, she pulled out her normal cell and sent a brief text to her husband.

She and her husband, Captain Michael Spinner, have been married for nearly twenty years, but spend only a fraction of that time inhabiting the same space together. As the commanding officer of the *USS Michael Monsoor,* one of the Navy's three Zumwalt-class guided missile destroyers, Captain Spinner was currently at sea, somewhere in the Gulf of Oman. Sent there one month ago, along with 18 other warships as a visible show of force to Iran and the Houthis. When he's not at sea, the ship's home port is on the left coast, in San Diego.

Prior to his current deployment, his ship needed quite a bit of time for sea trials. The Zumwalt class incorporates the Navy's bleeding edge stealth design and weapons technology. The *Michael Monsoor* was only the second of seven of this new class of destroyer to be built, and there were a lot of bugs to work out, requiring Captain Spinner to remain with his ship, rarely making it back to DC.

Both of their jobs leave little time for their relationship. But since she's married to politics and now the White House and he's married to the Navy, it's an arrangement that suits them perfectly. Neither are particularly interested in having children, something they easily agreed on from the start. But they do call, write emails, and text each other almost daily.

For them, distance is ironically a boon to their relationship—it allows them to consistently be the best versions of themselves with each other. Gone are the petty squabbles, irritating quirks and annoying idiosyncrasies that tend to wear on most couples who live in close, daily proximity.

Missing are the anxiety fueled mood swings that tend to come with their high-octane, high-stress jobs and lives. They get to maintain the perfect images they hold of each other without the dilution and disillusion that reality tends to trigger for most couples.

She was in the middle of one of those anxiety fueled moods right now.

It was time. She picked up her burner and dialed. On the first ring, "Hello, Madame Vice President."

"Hi, Courtney. We have a situation. Or at least I believe we do."

"Whatever you need."

"I need you to find out if Eve Tuant is here in DC."

"Living or visiting?"

"Not sure."

"I'll run her name. If I come up dry, I'll fly to Boston. Confirm her whereabouts."

"If she's here, she's probably using an alias. She was Elise Wainwright when she met with Senator Trahison. I doubt she'd use it again, but you never know."

"I'll check it."

"She's also been meeting with the president, but definitely not at the White House. I'd like to know where."

"Once I locate her, I can track her. Then what?"

"I need to know what she knows. Don't care how. Then. Well… you know what's next."

"Got it. Put some funds in the account. I'll need some help. Especially when it comes time to get her."

"How much?"

"Hundred and fifty k should do it."

"Seems like a lot."

"Pros cost."

"Fine. Done."

"That it?"

"I'll call in a week for updates."

"'Talk then." The line went dead.

She powered off the phone, removed the battery and dropped both into her purse as her normal cell pinged. It was a long, warm, and funny text from her husband that belied the conversation that had just ended.

She didn't answer him right away. She'd need some time to mentally and emotionally pivot.

She wasn't a machine, after all.

Although, in the stillness of her frequent three a.m. awakenings—mind coiled, sleep routed—staring blindly into the enveloping inky blackness, some nights she can almost hear her heart hardening.

Chapter 13

Eve watched through her night vision binoculars as three men emerged from the mosque's front door more than 300 yards away. "Right on time, gentlemen," she whispered to herself. Each was wearing a white prayer cap that glowed a pale, ghostly green in her lenses, and salwar kameez, the traditional Afghan full-length shirts and trousers, as they walked toward her.

She placed the binoculars on the ground next to her so that she could peer into the sight mounted to the top of her FN SCAR MK17. It too was set to night vision mode. She had opted to attach the 20-inch barrel to this Belgian-made battle rifle, giving her a range of more than 900 yards, not knowing how much distance she'd end up needing.

But she found that the primary position she had scouted two days earlier was open and clear. She was on a slight hill north of the mosque with an unobstructed view of the street as she lay prone under the cover of a mature, sprawling Rose of Sharon bush in full, thick bloom. The sweet but faint fragrance of the four-inch pink blossoms had an additional calming effect as she steadily sighted-in her target. With the longer barrel, she had much more range than she'd need. *All the better to kill you with, my dear.*

Her primary target was the man walking in the middle,

Arman Sarbaz, a tribal leader who had sided with the Alliance to fight the Taliban. But Eve and her team had recently discovered he was serving as a double agent. He was personally responsible for feeding the Taliban with operations plans that had led to three ambushes that caused heavy casualties, including seven US soldiers.

But that was about to end. Right here. Right now.

She squeezed the trigger. A fraction of a second later, from the quiet and flashless report of her suppressed muzzle, most of the back of Sarbaz's head exploded as the soft-point, 7.62-millimeter round expanded as it passed through. She quickly got the man on his left in her crosshairs before he realized what was happening and he met the same fate. The man on the right dove to the ground, which is where Eve's last shot found him. As the bullet hit him, an alarm sounded—an incessant, steady beeping—and she awoke.

The sound was coming from her phone. Noting that it was 3:14 a.m. as she picked it up, it was the security alarm she had installed in her Boston loft apartment. And she was now looking at a man closing the front door behind him.

The high-end security system was installed by a CIA associate shortly after she moved in. It's not that she was paranoid or fearful, but given the nature of her work, it was simply the prudent thing to do. Most of her colleagues followed the same protocol. The system had no visible control panel, her phone served that role, so there was nothing onsite that indicated a security system was in place. Twelve night-and-day vision cameras were peppered among the inset lighting, so that at first glance the cameras and lights were indistinguishable, especially if the lights were left off, which they now were. Seven additional, very small, wide-angle cameras were extremely well hidden in the walls. The placement and angle of every camera meant the entire loft was visually covered.

Her intruder stood still for a few moments before turning on a small, high-intensity flashlight and started walking around. Sitting on the edge of her bed as she watched, her phone recording it all, she said "And who might you be, my slinky friend?" His ghostly gray face was quite clear. "Smile, you're on *Candid Camera*, fucker."

Now that she was fully awake and sleep would be impossible, she put on her robe and carried the phone into the kitchen, started a pot of coffee while she continued watching. Her intruder was making his way through the main floor. His flashlight roamed across her rolling painting table that held a skyline of bottles, jars and tubes of paint, three coffee cans filled with brushes and palette knives—several stretcher bars and a long roll of raw canvas leaned against one end. He opened the large drawer in the table's center, rifled through with his rubber-gloved hands then closed it.

The way he moved and the areas he lingered over indicated that this was no amateur. He had done this before. No doubt. "I can't wait to find out who you are, shithead," she muttered to the screen as she scooped coffee into the filter basket. He went through the entire main level, looking through the two clothes and storage closets, all the kitchen drawers and cabinets and the bathroom cabinets before making his way up the open, wide oak stairs that led to the loft's bedroom.

With the flashlight held in his mouth, he went through each of the six drawers of her dresser, held up a pair of her thong underwear and examined them for a few moments and held them to his nose for a second before putting them back. "Perve," she muttered. "Just for that, I'm gonna find out if you're a boxers or briefs guy." He then went through the single drawers on the night tables on each side of the bed. Then back down the stairs through the main living area as he scanned the room, his light moving across the entire space one last time before leaving, thirty-five minutes later.

She was relieved but not surprised that he didn't find her hidden safe. Not that he could have done anything to it. It was a GSA Class 5 with an X-10 lock made by Brown Safe specifically for military and embassy use. This nearly unbreachable, 725-pound beast sat inside a three-foot tall and wide, black wooden box that served as the pedestal base for the nude sculpture of Eve that her good friend Paige Bradley had created years ago when they both attended the Pennsylvania Academy of Fine Arts.

She and Paige had become close friends and roommates during the two years they spent together at the Academy and Eve easily agreed to model for this incredible piece and several others. In fact, Eve became Paige's favorite model. And she was deeply moved when Paige gifted it to her after graduation.

It was one of the rare works in wood that Paige had created. She told Eve that she found the medium unforgiving and preferred to work in clay that was then cast in bronze. Eve was not only grateful to receive such an amazing gift, but she was also grateful the nearly life-size sculpture was wood and not bronze. It meant she could lift it to hide and access her safe.

Not wanting to wake him so early, Eve waited another two-and-a-half hours before she texted Leo, using his new app for the first time. He had ingeniously hidden it in plain sight among her phone's array of apps by using the American Airlines icon, which even opens the airline's home screen. It then uses a biometric authenticator to start sending and receiving the highly encrypted text messages.

She made an English muffin with peanut butter, her usual breakfast, ate it as she finished her coffee, then dressed and headed out to Langley.

Chapter 14

Eve thought she'd beat the typical morning DC commute as she made her way to Langley but was a bit surprised to see how many cars were out and about this early and arrived at Leo's office door an hour later. She turned the knob, found it locked and knocked. Leo opened it moments later. "You lock it now?" she asked as she stepped in.

"Yup. As soon as you brought me into this."

"Ah. Wise move."

As they settled into the large space that had six cubicles and a sizeable desk by the back wall, Eve asked, "Is this whole office yours?"

"It is. It had been used by a cyber security team that outgrew it. I've just not bothered to remove the cubes and desks. And I find working at different ones from time to time breaks up the monotony a bit when I'm here and not in the field… So whatcha got?"

Eve held her phone and played the security footage for him. As he plugged a wire into her phone he said, "Let me download this and run it through the Agency's facial recognition software and we'll see who your new friend is."

"I'm not only pissed that he went through my loft, but he woke me in the middle of a great op memory dream."

"Which one?"

"Arman Sarbaz."

"Arman Sarbaz…Wait, was he the traitor? Alliance guy who actually batted for the other team? Served up our operations plans to the Taliban, right?"

"That's him."

That went pretty well as I recall. Yes?

"As close to perfect as they get."

"You never told me how you found out he was a traitor."

"Leveraged a relationship I had developed over a couple months with one of the women who worked as a cook in his household, which was a typical Afghan compound. Once we suspected he was the intelligence leak, a couple times a week, dressed in full burka, I'd serve meals and tea to him and his frequent guests. It still amazes me how invisible women are in 'Stan. How insignificant we are in their eyes. Like we're not even human. The advantage to that attitude is that they'll say anything to each other in our presence.

"One night he disclosed the details of an op to two men I hadn't seen before and assumed were Taliban. We had planned the op only two days prior. While they were sipping their tea, he told them everything. And he did it with such ease that he could have been describing his last game of buzkashi. So that op was cancelled and his fate sealed. Took him out three nights later."

"Sweet… I never could figure out the rules to buzkashi. No matter how many times I watched. Just a bunch of crazy guys on horses going every which way. And how fucked up on opium do you have to be to invent a game that uses a headless goat?"

"Sarbaz could have been a goat substitute after I was done with him."

She stepped over to the cubicle with the computer she

used last time. "While you're doing that, I'm gonna check on Harrison's mail."

"Already turned it on for you."

"Thanks!" She sat in front of the monitor and started clicking away. Five minutes later, "Well, well, well. Guess who's getting a letter from Earthworks, today?"

"Perfect timing. Wiretap's in place. Whoa, that was fast."

"I know, right?"

"Not that, this. Come see who your underwear admirer is."

Eve scurried over and pulled a chair next to Leo. "Yup. That's him alright. Courtney Collins. Or at least that's his name today. He's also been Gerald O'Brien, Shawn Dempsey, and Liam Quinn. Holy shit. Look at that rap sheet. Starts in '93. Member of the Provisional Irish Republican Army. At the tender age of twenty, Quinn, apparently his real name, is suspected of planning the Shankill Road bombing. Nine killed when a bomb prematurely exploded at a fish shop in Belfast. They were supposed to blow up a meeting of loyalist paramilitary leaders in a room above the shop. But Liam and his IRA friends apparently didn't know the meeting had been rescheduled and the bomb went off anyway."

"Ouch. Talk about not gettin' the memo."

Eve's phone started ringing. Picking it up, she said, "It's Captain Evans… Hey, Bill, wassup?"

"Wanted to let you know some guy came to the station yesterday, late afternoon, asking about you. Slight but noticeable Irish brogue. My Spidey-sense went off when I saw him."

Eve said, "Six-feet tall, blue eyes, brown hair, buzz-cut with graying temples, salt-and-pepper goatee, four-inch scar around his left eye?"

"Yup. Friend of yours?"

"Your Spidey sense is still sharp, Bill. He's a bad fucker. Got him on camera breaking into my loft last night."

"Shit! I'll put out and APB and pick him up."

"Actually, no. Don't. We think he may be connected to the cabal somehow. Don't want him spooked. Not yet anyway. Looking at the highlights of his rather lengthy rap sheet as we speak."

"Got it. He didn't get shit from us. Told him that as far as we knew, you were still in town. That you sometimes travelled for art shows."

"Thanks, Bill."

"Should we keep an eye on your place?"

"No need. He won't be back."

"Okay. I know you can handle yourself, but keep your head down, Eve. And let me know of anything you need on our end."

"Will do, Bill. Thanks."

"Bye, Eve."

Leo said, "He's wants to know where you are."

"Tells me he's probably connected to Robin Spinner. She got spooked hearing my name. Thing is, very few people know that I'm connected to Homeland. Even fewer know that police station was where Boston's Homeland team meets. Not even the press sussed it out. Tells me he's hard-wired in. Ticks another box for our VP. What else we got on this fucker?"

"Brits lost track of him for several years. Disappeared until the FBI connected him to the Irish mob here in the states. Some years in Chicago, then more in Boston. ATF got involved in 2001. Seems Liam, Shawn Dempsey at the time, was running guns and explosives from Boston to his IRA buds in Belfast. Our friend here was suspected of being behind the BBC bombing that year. But MI5 couldn't prove it. Since no one was hurt or killed, they didn't press very hard to find him."

Still looking at the screen, Eve added, "Damn. While he changed his name to Gerald O'Brien, he certainly retained his taste for dealing weapons. FBI tagged him as a suspected weapons connection to the Russian mob, Hell's Angels, several nasty third-world dictators, and Iran. What the fuck!"

Leo said, "Iran's been using Hell's Angels to hit ex-Iranian military and other critics living in the U.S. They tried to whack an Iranian journalist just up the road in Maryland last year. She'd been writing criticisms of the country's supreme leader."

"Why the hell is someone like this going through my loft?"

An impish smile, Leo said, "Perhaps he thinks your thong can be weaponized."

"He's not wrong. But only when I wear them... Seriously. What's Quinn's, aka Courtney Collins' connection to all of this?"

"It's your call, Eve, but I think we should wiretap the VP's phones sooner than later. They just amped up the threat a buncha notches."

"Okay. Do it. Tap her cell. One of these other numbers could be her burner. Once we know for certain we can listen in there, too. I'll let the president know what we're doing when we meet next."

As he handed her a tiny, white cardboard box, he said, "Got one more thing I need you to do."

She opened it to a pair of red garnet stud earrings with sterling silver settings and posts and said, "Leo, you shouldn't have. This mean we're going steady?"

"No, but they do emit a steady signal. Just squeeze the earring back and stone together. You'll feel the slight click to activate them. Both have a GPS chip, so it doesn't matter which one. Or hit both just to be sure. And garnet's your birthstone, right?"

"Yes. January. You've really thought this through, haven't you? But do you think it's necessary?"

"Look, I know you're tough. Seen it firsthand. But we're neck deep in some pretty serious shit here. I was going to give you these before Unlucky Charms here broke into your place. Now I'm even more convinced we need all the insurance we can get. You've kicked a giant hornet's nest wide open. And these are Murder Hornets, Eve."

"Thanks, Leo. Read an article in the *Washington Post*, a month or so ago. The Hmong people in Viet Nam consider eating Murder Hornets a delicacy."

With a wry smile, she added, "I see some Vietnamese take-out in our future."

Chapter 15

Chief Justice Harrison was at his desk when his burner phone rang. Right on time.

"Good morning, Madame Vice President," he said after the fourth ring, not wanting to appear too servile.

"Good morning, Mister Chief Justice. I see your prediction about the Chevron ruling was accurate. Six-to-three vote. Nicely done."

"Thank you. Chevron's defeat paves a regulatory path we can begin to leverage. On an unrelated note, did you see yesterday's story in the *Times*?"

"Been a bit preoccupied. What in particular?"

"Looks like President Atout left me with another turd to deal with. When Justice Kelvan was being vetted by the Senate, if you recall there were some allegations of sexual misconduct. At the time the Idiot in Chief claimed to the press and spouted all over social media that he was giving the FBI free reign to investigate."

"And?"

"Turns out he did just the opposite. Senator Whitestone, the Judiciary Committee member who was Kelvan's most vocal opponent, just provided the *Times* with highly damning evidence of Atout's extremely tight control over the investigation. And messages to the FBI tip line forwarded to the White House were ignored. There were 450 of them."

"Shit. What'd the FBI say?"

"Declined comment."

"Figures. Well, he's been on your court for what, five years now? Extremely unlikely he'll be going anywhere. It may look bad at the moment, but honestly, with all the shit that's hitting the fan about the first anniversary of the Greater Boston Massacre, the growing outcry for a Congressional hearing, Ukraine and Russia, and the upcoming election, it probably won't go further than a single news cycle."

"Perhaps. But it certainly adds fuel to the opposition's vociferous demands and proposals for a formal code of ethics and term limits for my Court."

"When I'm in control, this will join so much other detritus I plan to sweep under the Oval Office rug. What're you focusing on next?"

"*Corner Post versus Federal Reserve* should be on the docket."

"Which is?"

"It puts the six-year statute of limitations to file challenges to longstanding regulations into play"

"Outstanding! Leverages Chevron."

"Indeed. Eliminating the statute of limitations could effectively open up all regulations to challenges. Regardless of how long they've been on the books. We could potentially rewrite decades of law."

"Brilliant! This is the kind of news I really needed to hear, Douglas. It's been a taxing few days."

"Unusually so?"

"It looks like Eve Tuant may be here in DC and meeting with the president."

"Shit. That's not good. No. That's not good at all."

"Confirming her whereabouts as we speak."

"Highly unsettling. She's a huge threat. Damn it! You'll keep me in the loop."

"Of course."

"She could end both of our careers. Our freedom. Perhaps our lives."

"I'll handle her. Don't worry about it. Just keep doing what you're doing, Mr. Chief Justice. Leave her to me."

"Certainly. But I want to remain informed."

"Tell you what, Douglas. Let's communicate on this day and time every week for the foreseeable future. How does that sound?

"That helps."

"Good. Just keep your phone off and the battery out in the meantime."

"Will do. Thank you, Robin."

"Don't give Eve Tuant a second thought. She will not get in our way again. You have my word. We'll talk soon. Bye."

"Bye," he said as he continued to ponder this new information. Assurances aside, he was still going to worry. If Eve Tuant was here and meeting with the president, then he had plenty of fodder for anxiety.

Sure, she could be here for other reasons. She's a seasoned CIA officer, after all. Quite adept at her job, from what he experienced firsthand and was able to glean, mostly from word of mouth. Not even Chief Justices had access to the CIA's inner sanctum. And there are certainly any number of global situations that would warrant her well-honed counterintelligence talents.

But the Greater Boston Massacre was only a year ago. It still loomed large in everyone's mind, including his. And Tuant was the primary reason their carefully laid plan failed so miserably. So fatally. There's really no way to know what she may have learned from either Trahison. She was alone with both the uncle and nephew. And with Hunter Forte. Right up to the end. The end that came about by her own hand.

His finely tuned lawyer logic was telling him that it was very likely Tuant found out there were additional members of their small group of patriots. Others working with Forte and the Trahisons. Others who are also part of this deeply committed group dedicated to saving America from itself.

Although their numbers had diminished greatly since they started. Pretty much cut in half. He thought, *now there's only the vice president, someone she's got working with her and me. But wasn't it Margaret Mead who said, "Never doubt that a small group of thoughtful, committed citizens can change the world; indeed, it's the only thing that ever has."*

His lawyer logic reared its head again. *But that cuts both ways, doesn't it?*

———

She hung up the phone a bit surprised by the justice's level of concern over Eve Tuant-. It wasn't just what he said, it was the strain, close to panic, she heard in his voice. He was as rattled as she had ever heard him in all the years they'd known each other. She was glad he was so receptive to their talking every week. This way she could keep a finger on his pulse. She knew she could trust him. But people can become unpredictable under pressure. And pressure and unpredictability tend to be on a sliding scale.

Self-preservation is hard-wired, especially in politics.

She thought, *as politicians, we begin this job believing we'd be self-sacrificing heroes when the moment called for it. Mr. Smith goes to Washington-kind of heroes. But before long most of us come to learn that it's just not true. It's why we venerate the hero. The longer we become enmeshed in the grinding, shifting gears of politics, the more we realize we will only become heroes vicariously.*

After she hung up with the justice, she dialed another number. Courtney Collins answered on the first ring. "Good evening, Madame Vice President."

"Where're you now?"

"Boston. Back in DC tomorrow afternoon."

"And?"

"Tuant's definitely not here. From the looks of her place, she's been gone for a while. Few months, maybe."

"Shit. Was afraid of that. What now?"

"Now I tap some low friends in high places. DC Metro detective I know. Traffic cams will find her. You said she meets with the president, but not in the White House?"

"Not that I've seen."

"Doesn't the White House keep a log of his trips? Secret Service goes wherever he goes. Can't you find out where? You are VP, after all."

"I hung around and kept an eye out when he told his secretary he'd meet Tuant. He never left the building. Never got in his car. Perhaps they meet somewhere in the basement. Situation Room's down there. There's also a bunker, bowling alley, lots of other stuff like a flower shop, carpenter shop, a dentist's office, all kinds of storage rooms and some tunnels. Perhaps she gets in that way. Undetected. There's no way for me to find out without raising suspicion. You gotta locate her. And soon."

"What's the rush?"

"Olson is sending me on a whirlwind tour to the UK, Japan, and then Australia. I'll be gone for just over three weeks. I leave in two days."

"What for, if you don't mind me askin'?"

"AUKUS partnerships. Wants me hands-on. I'm going with State and the Joint Chief. While I welcome the opportunity, I'm a bit suspicious of the timing."

"Is AUKUS that Australia submarine deal that pissed France off so much? Cancelled their huge contract to sell the Aussies a bunch of subs, didn't it?"

"Yup. They're still pissed."

"They've got sixty-five billion reasons to be. Didn't Australia pay them over eight hundred million when they backed out of the deal?"

"Actually, we paid it. You seem to be up on your arms deals, Courtney."

"Just a passing interest of mine. Typical French. Once you get on their bad side, there's no comin' back."

"I'll still reach out to you while travelling. Just less frequently. And you can always do the same. I'll reply when I can."

"Shouldn't be a problem."

"I need to know what she knows."

"Like I said, no problem. That it? We good?"

"For now. Talk soon."

"Safe travels."

Chapter 16

Eve was sitting on her patio in a white metal chair with flowered cushions at a small, round metal table with a glass top. The patio was what swayed her to choose this apartment among her half-dozen available options. The sixty square-feet of tile surrounded by an airy metal railing made her 700-square-foot space feel that much larger, even during the cold months since it was visible through the twin French doors and large windows of her open-concept apartment. The patio held the promise of warm days like this.

The morning sun splashed across the newspaper she had spread next to her coffee cup and a small plate that contained the crumbs of an English muffin. While most of her contemporaries got their news through their phones and tablets, she still preferred the tactile touch of a newspaper and the smell of ink.

A smell that was at the moment fighting with the skunky odor of marijuana that wafted in the warm July breeze. *Wow,* she thought, *someone's smoking their breakfast. Weedies, breakfast of champions.*

Her phone pinged and pulled her attention away from a story covering Ukraine's latest attempt to counter Russia's advances and her reminiscences of the last time she was there two years ago. She went to present to President Zelenskyy and his generals a CIA counterintelligence analysis and a corresponding offensive strategy that she had developed.

Leo was texting her.

She opened her American Airlines app, pressed her right index finger to the screen's biometric circle and read, *Get here as soon as you can. Wiretap scored a double header.* She replied, *See you soon!* He texted, *Don't leave without putting on a hat. Keep it on until you get here. You'll see why.* She was puzzled but replied with a thumb's up emoji.

She dressed quickly, rummaged through her closet for her Red Sox baseball hat and put it on as she went out the door.

She was knocking on Leo's office door forty-five minutes later.

After Eve read the transcript of both conversations, she said, "Now we know who two of the burner phone numbers belong to. The Chief Justice and VP. Makes sense. But this third number, not on our list, is definitely Collins. How on earth did he and Spinner get connected? Doesn't sound like she knows about his background as an arms dealer."

"I'm still coming to grips with the fact that this is the Chief Justice of the Supreme Court we're talking about," Leo said.

"You were right about the strategic shift to use the courts to impact and control the states."

"Would've been happy to be wrong."

"Thanks for the hat tip, but I'm not going to hide. They'd locate me eventually, anyway."

"I see you're not wearing the earrings I gave you."

"First thing I'll do when I get home."

"Now that we know who we're dealing with," Leo said, "let's turn the tables a bit."

"How so?"

"I can also access every traffic camera in the country from

here. I'll run an ongoing facial recognition algorithm for Courtney Collins. Concentrate on DC, but he'll be flagged wherever he goes."

"Good. I'm going to turn up the heat on our Chief Justice. I think he's primed."

"He does seem rattled by you."

"Let's shake that tree and see what falls out. Also, I'm assuming you now have a wiretap on Courtney's phone."

"I do."

"Can we include the personal cells of all three as well?"

"Already done."

"My hero."

"Thinkin' about getting a cape."

"Okay, but no tights, please."

"No worries. Don't have the legs for 'em"

"Promise?"

"Cross my heart and hope to fly."

Chapter 17

The mood was subdued, matching the gray sky. And the crowd was contained, consisting mainly of state and local government officials, a few invited guests, and many members of the Press from all over the country and parts of the world. There were more cameras than people.

The decision to keep the crowd small for the first anniversary observance of the Greater Boston Massacre was made for one reason—the ground was still considered hallowed and the number of people walking on it had to be kept to as few as possible.

The President stood at the microphone-quilled lectern that had been set up in Everett, very near to ground zero. The area was still a barren moonscape. Much of the gray dust and ash stood in long rows of massive fifty-foot-tall mounds, more like small mountains. The four-square-block area where the Greater Boston Massacre Memorial would soon begin to be dug and constructed was cordoned off by three-foot tall orange plastic fencing. The temporary concrete-making operation, with its large, elevated tanks connected by ramps of conveyer belts, stood as silent sentinels next to the ash mountains.

Eve and the rest of the world watched on their television monitors, tablets, and cell phones. President Olson had declared this a National Day of Observance, so all businesses and schools were closed. It would become so in perpetuity. Written into the national calendar, forever etched in the nation's soul. Every flag on every government building hung at half-mast. Public digital billboards, monitors and screens that hung in places like Times Square had turned off all advertising and were broadcasting only this event with scrolling banners listing every one of the more than 600,000 names of those who lost their lives. Since it would take more than sixteen hours for every name to be displayed, this had begun at 6:00 a.m. across all national broadcast stations. And nearly every cable and streaming service voluntarily followed suit.

Standing silent, stoic, slowly turning his head and absorbing his bleak surroundings for a few moments, the President stepped forward and began to speak.

"As I look around at this vast sea of hallowed ground today, the day we venerate the first anniversary of the largest loss of life on American soil since the Civil War, this day of heartbreaking infamy, I see more than mile upon mile of desolate, scorched earth that has become the final resting place for six-hundred and five-thousand, three-hundred and twenty-two souls. I see a crossroad. Not just these roads in front, behind and around us that connect Everett and East Boston, Chelsea and Malden and Somerville and each of the remaining list of cities and towns that have been decimated by the tragedy that befell this place a year ago today.

"I see a crossroad for America.

"We are not here because of the heinous act of some foreign enemy. If that were the case, while the end result would not have changed, the heartache would be less severe. No, we are not here because of a global adversary hell bent on punishing America. We are here because *we* are the enemy. *We* are the antagonist in this heart-rending story, this tale of avarice, self-centeredness, and narcissism.

"When George Washington gave his farewell address on September 17th in 1796, it contained an uncanny prophesy. That here, 230 years later, we are witnessing its fulfillment. He said, quote, 'The common and continual mischiefs of the spirit of party are sufficient to make it the interest and duty of a wise people to discourage and restrain it. It serves always to distract the public councils and enfeeble the public administration. It agitates the community with ill-founded jealousies and false alarms, kindles the animosity of one party against another, foments occasionally riot and insurrection. It opens the door to foreign influence and corruption, which finds a facilitated access to the government itself through the channels of party passions. A fire not to be quenched, it demands a uniform vigilance to prevent its bursting into a flame, lest, instead of warming, it should consume.' End quote.

"We *have* become this unwise community of ill-founded jealousies and false alarms. We *have* kindled the animosity of one party against another. And we *have* fomented riot and insurrection. But instead of opening the door to foreign influence and corruption, this was an interior door.

"We opened this door from the inside.

"And, yes, it is to our great shame that we *have* failed to keep our vigilance. Vigilance that would have prevented its bursting into a flame that was undeniably *not* a warming one, but instead a fire that *did* consume. With vehemence. Ferocity. And unprecedented fatality.

"I know you are all looking for resolutions to the many unanswered questions that remain about this devastating event. Did the perpetrators we already know about have any other allies? If so, who are they? Where are they? I am also looking for these answers. And I will not stop; I will not rest until these, and every other burning question are quenched by answers. You have my solemn oath. Mark my words. So, I will say this regarding any remaining enemy from within, to those who may be connected to this tragedy in any way. If you are listening to my voice, know this whoever you are—we will find you. There is no place on earth, above or below this earth, that is safe for you. You will be found. And justice will be served. Swiftly. Unreservedly. I swear on all that is holy, your days are indeed numbered.

"So, I say again, America is at a crossroad. The question is which direction will we choose today? Which path into the future will we follow? Shall we continue down the path of division and discord that has had its full measure borne out here in this place? Or can we take a different path? An older, well-worn path.

"A path that leads to a time when our political differences took a backseat to our shared humanity, our common good. Where reasonable compromise was the bellwether. Where the interests of the people over the interests of party was the common denominator—that what was best for every American, not just for those with my political label, was the factor used to measure every equation's balance.

"I think the choice is quite clear. Look around at this scorched earth. Let this visage sink into our collective being, into our collective souls, and into our collective memories. See where the path we have been on has led us. Listen to the six-hundred and five-thousand, three-hundred and twenty-two voices who are crying out to every American heart and soul, singing with one chorus the words, *never again*. Please, never again.

"America is at a crossroad. Which way will you choose today?

"I'll leave you with some hard-gained wisdom spoken by our sixteenth President. On the afternoon of November 19th in 1863, Abraham Lincoln spoke these words at Gettysburg, only four hundred miles from here, where the ground was also deeply hallowed.

"To a grieving, profoundly wounded nation, he said, quote, 'From these honored dead we take increased devotion to that cause for which they here gave the last full measure of devotion; that we here highly resolve that the dead shall not have died in vain; that the Nation shall under God have a new birth of freedom, and that governments of the people, by the people and for the people shall not perish from the earth.' End quote.

"And so, I say to you today, these dead shall also not have died in vain. And that we shall indeed continue to be a government, of, by, and for the people which shall not perish from the earth. So help us God."

The screaming engines of four F15 Eagles flying only one-thousand feet above could be heard before they appeared at the right side of the gathered assembly. As they flew overhead, the third jet pulled up and out of the formation, performing the Missing Man Flyby.

As a bugler finished playing Taps, Eve's eyes were so full of tears, she had trouble finding the remote on the coffee table to turn off her flat-screen TV.

Chapter 18

Eve was wearing a pair of black dress yoga pants, *great in a fight or a need to run,* and a burgundy satin button-down shirt, nicely complementing her new garnet stud earrings. And even though it was a warm July evening, she added her beige blazer, mostly to hide the Glock 19 she had holstered at the back of her right hip. And while her five-inch stilettos would be a knockout choice for a night out, she decided on her black ballet flats, *also great in a fight or a need to run.*

The traffic to Alexandria was light and the trip took only twenty minutes. She found a spot on Duke Street, three houses down from Chief Justice Harrison's home, and parked. As she walked toward the house, the warm, humid breeze carried an intoxicating waft of roses in full bloom poking out from the entire front-yard fence of a house across the street.

Since the U.S. Marshals Service, and not the Secret Service, is tasked with providing security for Supreme Court justices, she had reached out to a Department of Justice contact to send word to the marshals guarding the Chief Justice's house that she'd be stopping by around this time.

So, when she reached the tall, black metal gate leading to Harrison's front walkway and was approached by a marshal who had emerged from an unmarked car parked out front, she had her Homeland ID out and showed him before he could ask. He said, "Ah, yes. We were told to expect you, Ms. Tuant. Are you armed, Ma'am?"

Boy, he's cute, she thought as she replied, "Yes, I am." *Really cute.*

"I'll need to hold your weapon while you're inside. You'll get it back on your way out." *Really, really cute.*

As she handed it to him, she smiled and said, "I know how many bullets there are. Better be the same amount when I come back."

He tried not to smile, but failed as he said, "Yes, Ma'am."

Eve walked toward the front door of the stately two-story house, painted deep blue with white trim. Black shutters bracketed all five windows. Yellow light diffused by white window drapes lit much of the brick walkway and flowered front yard. A patinaed copper lantern hung to the right of the front door above the house numbers; below them a black oval plaque with raised white letters that read, "Historical Alexandria Foundation" around the edges and "1830" in the center. Proof that she was indeed in the heart of what was known as Old Town Alexandria.

She went up the two brick steps and rapped the brass knocker attached to the center of the black oak door and waited. Moments later Mrs. Harrison answered the door—a handsome woman in her mid-fifties, bright pale-blue eyes set beneath her short brown hair. "Yes, can I help you?" She shot a quick glance behind Eve and noted the Marshal standing by the gate, watching.

Eve, holding up her Homeland ID, said, "Good evening, Mrs. Harrison. I'm Eve Tuant from Homeland Security. I know this is a bit of a surprise imposition, but I'm hoping to see your husband. It will only take a moment, I promise."

"Let me see if he's available. Please, come in." She stepped into the bright hallway, eggshell-white walls with bright white wainscoting and trim, polished dark oak floors. A long mahogany sideboard against the right wall—a Dolan marble table lamp, an antique Chinese sculpture of a horse and a fresh arrangement of summer flowers in a crystal vase on top. The smell of a roasting chicken wafted from an unseen kitchen. "Please wait here," she said as she made her down the hallway and entered a room to the right.

Eve could hear a muffled conversation. A man's voice that rose higher as he spoke. She couldn't make out what was being said, only the very terse tone, and suppressed a wry smile.

Mrs. Harrison came back into the hallway, closed the door behind her and walked briskly toward Eve looking a bit flustered. "I'm so sorry, Ms. Tuant. My husband is on a very important phone call, one of several scheduled and can't possibly see you this evening."

She reached behind Eve for the door and began opening it as she added, "He asked that you contact his judicial assistant to set up another meeting. But that could also take a while. With the Court in the midst of so many emergency stay requests, he does have quite a bit on his plate, as you can well imagine. I'm sorry, but I'm sure you understand."

"I do indeed, Mrs. Harrison. Thank you for your time. Have a good evening."

"Thank you. You as well."

Eve's smile was nearly ear-to-ear when she reached the gate that was being held open by the marshal who let her in. He said, "That was quick. But looks like it went well."

"It went perfectly."

As he handed her gun back, "All the bullets are there. Want to count 'em?"

"I trust you Marshal… what's your name?"

"Grant," as he handed her his card.

"I trust you." Looking at the card, "But if I do find any missing, I know who to call, Deputy Marshal Clay Grant."

Smiling, "Please. Call anytime, Ms. Tuant. Anytime at all."

She smiled back, held his eyes and said, "Eve," as she slipped her gun into its holster and his card into her coat pocket. She could almost feel his eyes on her as she headed back to her car. She opened the door and looked up; he waved. She waved back and when she got behind the wheel, began humming, *I Shot the Sherriff,* and then out loud, "But I did not shoot the deputy."

She sent a short text to Leo before driving off.

Chapter 19

Courtney Collins was sitting in his favorite leather wingback chair in his sunroom, although the only light coming through the three walls of nearly floor-to-ceiling windows at this late hour was from the luminous full moon, sitting high and alone, like a giant white period punctuating the cloudless night sky. He had most of the windows open and the piquant fragrance of magnolia bushes in full bloom that surrounded this side of his house wafted through the room with each breeze.

A bronze Franklin floor lamp over his left shoulder lit the pages of his favorite book by his favorite author, Roddy Doyle's *The Commitments*. The dog-eared pages revealed his most beloved sections. Doyle's liberal use of Irish slang made Courtney feel at home no matter where in the world he was reading it. He thought the movie did a grand job of portraying the book. No surprise since Doyle also wrote the screenplay.

He was reading the chapter with a quote by the novel's main character, Jimmy Rabbitte, that he was quite fond of and could recite from memory—*Do you not get it, lads? The Irish are the blacks of Europe. And Dubliners are the blacks of Ireland. And the Northside Dubliners are the blacks of Dublin. So, say it once, say it loud: I'm black and I'm proud.* —when his cell phone vibrated next to his nearly empty glass of Connemara whiskey on the mahogany end table beside his right armrest.

Noting the caller he said, "Dia Duit."

"Dia is Muire Duit"

"So, what's up?"

"Found your girl. Traffic cams picked her up in Alexandria three nights ago. Tracked her to 15th Street in DC before they lost her."

"What apartments are on or near 15th?"

"The Woodward Building's right there. She may have parked in their garage. Why we lost her. But now we've got her plate number. I'll text it to you. She drives a new, black Subaru BRZ."

"Can you run a check of Woodward residents?"

"Already did. There's no Eve Tuant living there."

"Must be using another name. Great work, Jack. I'll take it from here. Will I see you next week?"

"I'll be there. Slán agat."

"Slán agat."

After Courtney ended the call, he dialed.

Robin Spinner didn't pick up. At her voicemail prompt he said, "Call me when you can." And hung up. He looked at his watch and added the thirteen-hour time difference with Japan. It was one o'clock in the afternoon there. Tomorrow.

She was already well into a day full of meetings. He wasn't sure when he'd hear from her, but it didn't matter. He knew what he needed to do next.

Chapter 20

Leo had texted Eve at 7:30 this morning, letting her know that the wiretap had captured two recordings and asking when she wanted to come in. She texted back; she'd be there about 10:00. She wanted to get in a run, then hit the gym, and hopefully avoid most of the DC morning commute. The Woodward had a decent gym, and she was feeling a more insistent tug to keep up her weight-lifting routine.

At 10:30, Leo and Eve were in his office having just finished listening to and reading the transcript to the first recording. Eve said, "Must be Gaelic they're speaking. The transcription software clearly had no clue."

"So, his friend on the Metro force is a fellow bogtrotter. The call came from an extension of their main number. Shouldn't be too hard to find out who he is."

"Let's put a pin in that for now."

"No problem. What I don't like is that they now know where you live, your car and plate number."

"That was inevitable. I just made it a bit easier."

"But why make it easy for these fuckers?"

"I want them to feel like they've got the upper hand. It'll make them overconfident. You and I both know that overconfidence causes arrogance. And arrogance is the quickest way to kick the calendar."

"I get it. But I don't like it. Just keep your head up."

"Always. What's next?"

"You're going to really like this one.

Chief Justice Harrison's conversation with the vice president was made at 8:00 a.m. this morning, which was 9:00 p.m. tomorrow in Japan. *Time zones. Tomorrow is today. Today was yesterday. Go figure.*

Eve listened and read along with the transcript.

RS: "Why so many messages, Douglas? You know I'm in Japan. If I'm not in a meeting, I'm in yet another social gathering, which typically involves a lot of eating and drinking. I don't know how the Japanese get anything done. I'm always tired and still jet lagged to boot."

DH: "Jet lag? You're complaining about jet lag? Really?! She came to my *house*! To my fucking front door, Robin! Goddamn it! God fucking damn it!"

RS: Tuant came to your house?"

DH: "Who the fuck else!"

RS: "What did she say?"

DH: "I have no idea! I didn't meet with her. Had my wife run interference. What the fuck does this mean, Robin? She must know something."

RS: "Not necessarily."

DH: "Bullshit! Who knows what either of the Trahisons told her. She may even know about you, too! You think of that? Shit! Shit! This is bad, Robin. Real fucking bad!"

RS: "Calm down, Douglas. I told you I'm taking care of this. You have to trust me."

DH: "You mean like Senator Trahison trusted you?"

RS: "That was a low blow, Douglas. You know I had no

choice. *We* had no choice. But we're nowhere near that here. Not even close."

DH: "Wish I had your confidence, Robin. She scares the shit out of me. I'm not making threats but know that I'm not going down alone."

RS: "Look, I told you I've got someone on it. He's extremely capable. I've known him for a long time. He'll take care of it. But you need to calm down. Be the immovable, unflappable model of jurisprudence that the world has come to know, Douglas. You are the Chief Justice of the Supreme Court. She's nobody."

DH: "Don't patronize me, Robin. She's not nobody. She's CIA. Clearly resourceful and intelligent. And relentless. We can't afford to underestimate her again."

RS: "I'm not. You'll see. It's getting late and I have to prepare for tomorrow's meeting, Douglas. Then we leave for Australia. Two hours more than Japan. Sixteen hours ahead of DC, so please keep that in mind if you want to reach out. And I'll reply as soon as I possibly can. You gonna be okay?"

DH: "Getting there. Venting helped. I'll be fine when Eve Tuant is no longer a concern."

RS: "Just keep focusing on the great work you're doing, Douglas. Leave Eve to me."

DH: "I'll try. Safe travels, Madame Vice President."

RS: "Thank you, Mr. Chief Justice."

"Wow," Leo said. "He's completely unhinged. You put the fear of God in him. Damn, girl!"

"Never knew the justice had such a potty mouth. And all I did was show up at his house. Wonder what he'd do if I sat in the front row of the Court's next oral argument?"

"He'd shit his robe. You going to do that?"

"Was thinking about it. But after hearing this, I don't need to. He's already ripe."

"Oh, he's beyond ripe. He's fallen off the tree. And rolled down the road all the way to crazy town."

"Wish I could wield that kind of power over every man I meet."

"Look, I'll say it again. These people are more dangerous than the Taliban we faced in 'Stan. Over there we usually knew where the bullets were coming from. This is different. We're talking some of the most powerful people in the country, if not the world. Keep your head on a swivel, Eve. Always."

"I will. And, like 'Stan, I've got you watching my back."

"Earrings look good on you."

"Thanks."

"No shocker there. You'd make a dumpster look good."

"You're not going to gift me with a dumpster now, are you?"

"Damn it. Way to spoil my Christmas surprise."

Chapter 21

Eve had left her apartment at the Woodward, once again heading north, and just as she was rounding the corner of 15th and H Street, running at a moderate pace, she noticed an SUV tailing her as she ran past the Dolly Madison House.

She was wearing her favorite black Athleta leggings and gray Nikes, but instead of her University of Toronto t-shirt, she had on her Boston Red Sox baseball jersey, since it more easily hid the Sig Sauer holstered to the small of her back. She not only favored the P365 as a backup gun due to its very small size, but she also liked its impressive ten rounds of nine-millimeter stopping-power that she further augmented with hollow points. While its three-inch barrel made it a relatively inaccurate weapon beyond fifteen yards, it kicked ass and erased names at close quarters.

As she entered Lafayette Square Park and ran past the statue of General Tadeusz Kościuszko, she sped up and turned her head slightly to catch two men scramble out of the car's back seat and scurry across H Street toward her. They were trying to be discreet but were clearly not anticipating a foot pursuit. They certainly weren't dressed for it. In fact, even though Eve only got a quick glance, they looked like bikers, motorcycle boots and all.

As she came to Andrew Jackson's statue at the center of the park, now running at a good clip, instead of taking the path that curves south leading to the Rochambeau statue across from 716 Jackson Place, where she was headed to meet with the president, she took the path that curved north.

In thirty feet, when she was on a portion of the path among a thick stand of trees and bushes, looking back and not seeing them, she hopped over a hedge of yews and went behind a large maple tree and peered around it. She had a clear view of the center of the park and the brick paths radiating from the circle around the Andrew Jackson statue.

The two bikers, clearly out of breath, stopped in front of the statue and looked around. She could hear one of them loudly say, "Fuck!" A young couple pushing a baby carriage nearby were a bit startled and annoyed when they heard it, but once they got an eyeful, did a quick right turn onto the path leading directly north as they picked up their pace. The two men spoke briefly to each other but were too far away for Eve to hear. One pulled out his cell phone and after a brief call they both headed back the way they came.

Eve watched as they left, waited a few more minutes and then, instead of getting back on the brick path, she went directly across it and made her way through the trees and shrubs, using the flowering crabapples, common boxwoods, pin oaks, silver maples, scotch elms, and horse chestnut trees as cover as she made her way to the Jackson Place sidewalk directly across from the Presidential Townhouse.

Before stepping from behind a large Korean ash, she watched a few cars go by and spotted the silver SUV that had been following her, slowly making its way down the street. She crouched low, hoping she couldn't be seen. She reached for her gun and held it at her side. Three men were scanning as they came closer. One looked in her direction, right at her, but didn't see her.

As they drove by, she noted the license plate number. After they continued to the end of Jackson, took a right onto Pennsylvania Avenue and were out of sight, she bolted across the street and up the brick townhouse stairs two at a time as she returned her gun to its holster.

As soon as she got to the door, it was opened by the same Secret Service agent who does so every time she comes, Steven Penn. He said, "That's an unusual way to arrive, Eve. As you know, we've got this street, all of Lafayette Square and much of the area covered by cameras. And we pay particular attention when the president is here. So, we noticed the guys following you, saw you hide and spotted the SUV moving down Jackson. How can we help?"

"Did you get their plate number?"

"We did. We'll run it and let you know what we find. Cameras also got a good look at their faces, so we'll run those, too. The president's waiting downstairs."

"Appreciate the help, Steven. Thank you. He hasn't been waiting long, I hope"

"About five minutes. And we just let him know what happened."

As she turned and trotted down the hall, "Thanks again, Steven! You're the best!"

The President stood from the sofa when Eve came in and gestured for her to join him as he sat. "Heard there was a bit of excitement on your way here."

"Yes, Mr. President. Kick a hornet's nest and angry hornets tend to come out."

She then let the president know that she and Leo decided to wiretap what they discovered was the vice president's burner phone, as well as her regular cell, and the two other connected burner numbers and their normal cells, now identified as belonging to Justice Harrison and Courtney Collins. She pulled the most recent call transcripts from her thigh pocket, unfolded and handed them to him.

After reading he said, "She pretty much admitted to killing Senator Trahison here. Although a good defense attorney could argue "had no choice" could mean something else. But there's no doubt."

"None, sir."

"I'm pissed about the Supreme Court now playing a key role in punishing the states that they don't like and helping the ones they do. But I must say I've never heard someone as distraught as the Chief Justice just because you visited his house. Wow.

"All of this is excellent evidence, Eve. Keep gathering it. Depending on how all of this unfolds, it will either inform the world, or at the very least it will inform the Senate and House intelligence committees. Then I'll see what can be done about these Supreme Court decisions. Some new legislation most likely. We are on completely unprecedented legal and Constitutional turf here. No doubt it'll keep the Justice Department and White House counsel busy for months. At the very least we should be able to craft some Executive Orders to counter or neuter some of this. Great work, Eve. Please extend my gratitude to Leo for me."

"I will, sir."

"Sending Robin to the other side of the globe hasn't had much impact on her ability to keep her fingers in the bitter pie she and the Chief Justice are making. Slowed her down a bit is about all. What's this Courtney person's story? Who is he?"

Eve told the president about his breaking into her Boston loft and filled him in on what they discovered about him and his past in Ireland, Chicago, and Boston and he said, "How the hell did Robin connect with a guy like that?"

"She told Harrison she's known him for quite some time. How they connected is still a mystery."

"Doesn't really matter much. But he's dangerous, Eve. No doubt he's behind you being followed just now. I'm very concerned for your welfare."

"I appreciate your concern, Mr. President, but this is what I wanted. I figured this would be the result of visiting the Chief Justice at his home."

"You've scared the bejesus out of him, Eve."

"It's what I was hoping for, sir. Better than I hoped. I want them reacting. I want them emotional. That's when they'll do something stupid. And I'll be ready. Dunce cap in hand."

"You said you spotted them as you ran by the statue of General Tadeusz Kościuszko?"

"Yes, sir."

"Did I ever tell you my Kościuszko story?"

Trying not to roll her eyes. "No, Mr. President, you didn't."

"Had you heard of him?"

"Not at all. First time I saw his name was on that statue. My American history is viewed through a Canadian lens, sir. Plus, whatever I needed to learn to gain U.S. citizenship. Like most, I'm familiar with the biggies, Washington, Lincoln, Jefferson and the like."

"Kościuszko and Jefferson became close friends. He came here from Poland in 1776. He was a godsend. A brilliant military architect. Oversaw the building of most of the Continental forts and fortifications, including West Point. But my story takes place in 1781. The Continental Army was attacking a British fort in South Carolina, called the "Ninety-Six.""

"Odd name. Was it their ninety-sixth fort?"

"No, it was ninety-six miles from the nearest Cherokee village. It was built many years before the British captured it. Anyway, Kościuszko, then a colonel, had the army dig trenches toward the fort so they could get closer while remaining under cover. He then built a thirty-foot tower so that they could shoot the Brits from above the fort walls. It was a brilliant tactic. Well, one day, while he was inspecting the trench, a British soldier bayonetted him in the ass."

"Oh, my. Painful, I'm sure. But how embarrassing."

"Indeed. In time he recovered from both wounds—his ass and his ego. As the war was drawing to a close in 1782, he led one of the last battles and beat the British outside Charleston, South Carolina. Continental Congress made him a brigadier general a year later."

"I'm surprised they didn't make him a rear admiral."

President Olson burst out in a loud, belly laugh that took him a minute to recover from. "Oh, my God, that's hilarious, Eve."

"I'll bet his soldiers laughed for a long time after."

"No doubt. Been nearly 250 years and we're still laughing."

"I'll never look at his statue quite the same way again, Mr. President. Especially from behind."

After he composed himself, he said, "Look, Eve, I'm worried. These people are playing for keeps. I can't officially give you Secret Service protection, but I can tell you that every one of the guys in this building would be at your side in a heartbeat. They almost ran out the door to help you a short while ago. Had something happened, they would have."

"Aww. I appreciate that, sir."

As if on cue, Steven Penn entered the room with a sheet of paper. "Excuse me, Mr. President, Eve. Got a hit on two of the guys in the SUV." He handed the paper to President Olson and after a quick scan he gave it to Eve. Steve continued, "The SUV was a rental." He points to one of the names on the sheet. "This one rented it."

Eve said, "Vincent Gianni, New York Hell's Angels chapter. The other is Frank Bateau, Quebec Hell's Angels. Seems Collins has a type."

President Olson said, "Quebec has a Hell's Angel's chapter?"

"Yes, sir. They're global. Chapters in much of the world."

"My image of Canadians is now tainted."

"It's branding, sir. We project nice, but we're still human. Dark underbelly and all. There was a big turf war in Quebec in the mid 90's to early 2000's. Often in the news. Quebec Hell's Angels pretty much had the monopoly on illegal drugs. Other dealers and crime families fought back. When it was all over, nearly 200 people were killed, 300 injured and 100 Hell's Angels incarcerated. Bateau was one of them. And it looks like Gianni did some time at Rikers. Extortion, drug dealing, prostitution."

"And these were the guys chasing you? Shit. Collins isn't screwing around. It tracks that he knows a lot of really bad people. I don't know if I should keep you on this thing, Eve."

"Look, Mr. President, I'm moved by your concern for me. I truly am. But I've faced death more times than I care to count. I've been shot five times, blown up once, tortured and beaten for two weeks, and nearly raped." Waving the piece of paper she added, "If anything, sir, you should be worried about these guys."

With an awestruck look on his face, he replied, "Duly noted."

Steven was still standing nearby. "Two questions. I guess that means you don't want an escort home?"

"You're kind, Steven, but no. Don't need one. The Woodward has gated and controlled access. It houses some of D.C.'s movers and shakers, so they do a pretty decent job with security. That said, it's still just an apartment building. Which is why I'm always vigilant."

"Second question. Should we pick these two up?"

Eve replied, "No. That would alert them. I want them clueless. Unaware that there's any possible threat. Completely oblivious.

"Like the goat that was set out for the tyrannosaurus rex in the movie *Jurassic Park*."

Chapter 22

The buzzing and vibrating burner phone on the nightstand next to Courtney's bed woke him. He never took the battery out, even though Spinner said he should. Didn't see the need. In his line of work, burner phones were his stock-in-trade and had never been an issue. As he reached for it, the digital clock next to it displayed 4:15 a.m. "Hello, Madame Vice President."

"Did I wake you? Never mind. Silly question. I just did the math... We've got a problem."

"What's up?"

"The justice has become highly unstable. Alarmingly so. Combustible even. Have you located Tuant?"

"Yes. She's living in the Woodward apartments, downtown on 15th. Had some guys follow her. She was running. Lost her in Lafayette Park."

"Do you think she saw them?"

"Not sure. I wasn't there. They didn't think so. They drove around some, but no luck. But now we can keep eyes on her place."

"Can't you do more than that?"

"We'll see. The Woodward has decent security. But I'm sure I'll find some holes."

"We may not have time for that."

"How come?"

"It won't take much for Harrison to crack wide open. Spill everything. He even said so. Tuant showed up at his house and he shit a brick. I've never seen him like this. If she confronts him, he'll fold like a paper napkin. I've been doing a lot of thinking about this for the last few days. The asset has become a liability. I hate the thought of losing him. He's already put a lot in motion. Some ground will be lost. Hope to gain it back when I appoint his replacement."

"Are you absolutely sure? There's no undoin' this."

"It's all I've been thinking about. So much so I spaced out in the middle of a meeting with the Australian Chief of Defense today. Blamed it on jet lag... Yes, I'm sure. You have a plan?"

"I do."

"And let me know when you have Eve. Got questions that need answers."

"On it."

"Sorry to interrupt your sleep."

"No worries. Why I make the big bucks."

"Talk soon."

"Bye, Robin."

———

Leo was awakened by his phone's pinging, letting him know that the wiretap had a new recording. Audrey, his girlfriend, stirred next to him as he picked up his cell, got up, padded down the hall to his study and closed the door. He turned on his laptop and logged into his CIA server through the Agency's VPN, the most secure network on the planet. He should know; he helped upgrade it.

He put in his earbuds, listened and then immediately texted Eve.

————

Eve was awakened by her phone. The text from Leo read, *She's planning to kill the chief justice. Warn his security. Come by tomorrow for the transcript.* She texted him back and told him when she'd be there.

She then got up and went to her closet. Reached into her blazer's pocket for Deputy Marshall Grant's business card and dialed his number. A groggy voice said, "Who the hell is this?" She tried not to picture him in bed. Naked. But failed.

"It's Eve Tuant."

His tone changed instantly. "Eve. A bit early to be looking for your bullets, isn't it?"

"Justice Harrison's life is in danger. I can't tell you any more than that. It's a real and imminent threat. How Homeland acquired this info is something I can't get into yet, Clay. But I will tell you that I'm also a CIA officer. Tighten his security. But keep it on the down low. He can't know. It's for his own good."

"Look, I hear you. But I don't really know you. I'd like to. I really would. But that's personal. How do I know I can trust this info?"

"Would you like to hear it from POTUS directly?"

"Get out. You're not serious."

"Dead serious. I can ask him to call you today."

"Ya, sure. Pull the other one. Okay, look, I know you're Homeland and believe you're CIA, so I'm taking you seriously, Eve. I'll get right on it. As soon as we hang up."

"When all of what I can't talk about right now comes to a

close, you may be hearing about a lot of it in the news. I'll fill you in on the rest. Over dinner, perhaps? You can choose the restaurant."

"Love the sound of that. Perhaps we can do so sooner? I'll bring the bullets."

Eve hung up and began to hum, *I Shot the Sherriff.*

Chapter 23

Courtney Collins was in the Starbucks on Second Street, half a block away from the Supreme Court building on this already hot and humid, early August morning.

But he looked like someone else.

One of the survival skills he had honed over a lifetime of living and working in the shadows was creating disguises. He had become quite adept at it.

One of the stories he tells only his closest, most trusted friends was the time he brokered a deal with the Mexican cartel Los Zetas for thirty M4 carbines, two M107 50-caliber sniper rifles and an M224 60-millimeter mortar. Once the deal was done, knowing the cartel's reputation for paranoia and brutally eliminating any potential loose ends, such as a lone arms dealer, Courtney dressed as a woman when he left his hotel for the airport.

His disguise was so convincing, one of the thugs the cartel sent to kidnap and kill him was standing by the front door waiting. He started hitting on Courtney as he awaited his taxi. When the thug pinched his ass as he was getting into the car, Courtney actually slapped him and called him a *cerdo* in his best Spanish and high-pitched voice. The thug smiled and made kissy faces at him as the cab pulled away.

Over the last few decades, he had not only convincingly

changed his gender, but he'd also changed his ethnicity, his age, and his race.

He always carried a small, black hard-shell case whenever he travelled the globe brokering deals. It was filled with pancake make-up of every skin tone, make-up brushes, hair dyes, a few bottles of nail polish, false eyebrows, eyelashes, sideburns, beards, mustaches, latex prosthetic noses, chins, ears, breasts, and various wigs. And bottles of liquid latex that he could form and shape into any body part or facial feature he wanted. Even a battery-powered mirror just in case he was in a location without electricity, which happened several times. And he always purchased local clothing wherever he went to help blend in with his environment—adding another layer to his chameleon camouflage.

Today he wore a white scraggly wig that poked out from a Washington Nationals baseball hat. His prosthetic nose made his own much bigger and had a small wart near the end of it, sprouting a couple of hairs. White bushy eyebrows poked above black-framed glasses. Fleshy foam latex jowls led to loose wattles of fake skin under his chin.

He looked a lot like Bernie Sanders.

As he stood at the kiosk that held the metal carafes of milk and half-and-half, a white sugar dispenser, a bin of brown sugar packets, a tray of coffee stirrers, napkins, and cardboard cup sleeves, he watched all four of Chief Justice Harrison's law clerks, two young men and two young women, as they stood nearby in a clutch chatting while waiting for their order. Two lattes, one Americano, one salted caramel cold brew and one cappuccino, which was what the justice drank every morning, with two packets of brown sugar.

Courtney surreptitiously emptied the brown sugar packet container into his left pants pocket. He took two nearly identical packets from his right pocket and cupped them in his hand.

One of the clerks, Jason Nevells, came over to the kiosk, gathered some stirrers and napkins and noticed the empty brown sugar container and said, "Shit, there's no brown sugar." Courtney, standing next to him, held up the two packets and said, "I don't need these, you're welcome to them."

Jason said, "You sure?"

"Absolutely." Pointing to his own cup, "Already added mine. These are extra."

"Thank you!"

"You are most welcome, young man. Have a wonderful day."

Courtney went out the door moments after they did and watched them head down Second Street toward the Supreme Court building, bantering and laughing as they went. He headed in the opposite direction toward Maryland Avenue, where his Uber would arrive shortly.

Chapter 24

Eve drove her car into The Woodward's underground parking garage and pulled into her assigned spot. It was a little after ten in the morning. She was returning from her meeting with Leo at Langley, where they listened to the wiretapped conversation between the vice president and Collins about killing the chief justice.

After listening to the recoding, she immediately opened Leo's app and texted the heart of the conversation to the president. She told him she had already contacted the U.S. Marshals, relayed the imminent threat and told them to increase security. He thanked her and asked her to relay his gratitude to Leo.

She was unable to get back to sleep after hearing from Leo and then contacting Deputy Marshall Grant. So, she was now tired and hungry. She had stopped at the Old Ebbitt Grill, an iconic DC eatery that was established in 1856 as Washington's first saloon. They had a great breakfast and brunch menu, most of which she had tried. And it was also conveniently located just up her street. The intoxicating aroma of steak and eggs emanating from the Styrofoam container in a white plastic bag on the passenger seat was calling to her. Loudly.

As she got out of the car, she noticed two men in blue work coveralls with white logos of an electrical contractor on their back. They were standing about forty feet away in front of a gray electrical box attached to the opposite garage wall, looking and gesturing at it, partially glancing her way a couple of times. Something seemed off. No work truck or van nearby. No tools. Scuffed motorcycle boots.

As she reached back into her car for the food, she pulled the Sig Sauer from her hip, thumbed the safety off and held it behind the bag. As she closed the door with her elbow and turned, both men were walking quickly toward her, and she immediately recognized them.

"Good morning, Vincent. Frank. Are the Hell's Angels in the electrical biz now?"

They were so taken back that they slowed, looked at each other for a moment, slack-jawed, wide-eyed, and then picked up their pace toward her. Vincent said, "You're coming with us." They were now just ten feet away. As they both reached into their coverall pockets for their guns, Eve said, "No I'm not."

She dropped her bag to put both hands on her gun and shot them before they could completely raise their weapons. But as Eve fired one round into each of them, center mass, Vincent, who was on her left, involuntarily squeezed his trigger while the gun was still in his pocket, pointing at a downward angle. The bullet hit Eve in the left foot. She felt a sharp burning pain as she fired two head shots, dropping them both in their tracks.

She popped her car's trunk and sat on the edge, unlaced her Doc Martin, pulled it off and removed her sock. While it was bleeding, she noted that the wound was small. But the pain was intense. It had hit the left side of her left foot with no exit wound, leading her to believe it was probably a .22-caliber round. She reached for the first aid kit she kept in her trunk. Always having one of these in every car she ever owned, rented, or leased was something her grandfather had drilled into her when he was teaching her how to drive. She could still hear his voice saying, "You just never know when you or someone else will need it. Could save a life."

After cleaning and wrapping the wound, she picked up her bag of food, took out her cell and dialed the DC Metro police. She then sat sideways in the tiny trunk, propped her leg up on the rear fender to elevate her foot. She then opened the bag, removed the container and some plastic utensils and began eating.

She offered some to Vincent and Frank. Neither replied.

Chapter 25

The chief justice and his four law clerks were sitting around the oak conference table that took up much of the outer office of the justice's chambers, finishing up their coffees. Harrison was pleased to see that it was starting out to be another lively day with these bright, sharp, rather recent law school grads. Each man and woman carefully culled from Yale and Harvard. Always two from each school. Whenever possible, one of each gender was selected.

He relished fueling the centuries-old rivalry between these two pillar law schools. It was the electricity that ran the justice's longstanding law clerk program. And, as he was first to admit, it juiced him, too.

Jason Nevells and Sarah Welsh graduated from Harvard Law three years ago, which was also when Edward Bushing and Christine DeMilla had graduated Yale's law school. While the chief justice is fed by the energy of his clerks, when he was being completely honest, their fealty wasn't hard to take either. Who doesn't love being in the same room for hours with four smart, funny, and fervent fans?

But no ass-kissing. Ever. Won't tolerate it. He encouraged healthy, open, unvarnished, unfettered opinions and brass-knuckled but respectful debate. And they were in the middle of one now.

They were discussing a Writ of Certiorari for *Spenser versus United States*, a case that came from the Seventh Circuit's court of appeals that was about gratuities. The issue in question was under what circumstances gratuities were actually bribes.

The case involved Albert Spenser, the former mayor of Danville, Indiana. He had awarded two contracts to a truck company to purchase five trash trucks for $1.1 million. The company then cut Spenser a check for $15K that he said was for consulting fees. The FBI investigated and the federal prosecutor charged him with accepting a gratuity for the contract. He was found guilty and sentenced to two years in prison.

His lawyer claimed that the law in question only criminalized bribes, but not gratuities. The appeals court affirmed Spenser's conviction, and he was now appealing to the Supreme Court.

Christine DeMilla was citing the law in question, 18 U.S.C. 666, a federal statute that President Reagan signed into law in 1984, when she noticed that the chief justice wasn't looking well. She stopped reading and asked, "Are you okay, Mister Chief Justice?"

His breathing was labored. He had become quite pale and was beginning to sweat profusely. "I'm not feeling so well." He clutched at his chest, his face contorted in a twisted grimace, "Fucking Spin—" was all he said as he fell face forward onto the table with a thud. "Holy shit!" Jason shouted as he and the rest rushed to the justice, "Who knows CPR?"

"I do!" answered Edward Bushing, who with Jason's help pulled the limp justice off the table by the shoulders. "Help me get him on the floor."

While Edward began chest compressions, Christine was already on the phone with the 911 dispatcher.

Five minutes later, the EMTs scrambled through the door and took over for Edward. They used the defibrillator on him several times before they lifted Harrison onto the gurney and rushed him out.

Edward, surrounded by his dazed, bewildered, and shocked colleagues, spoke in a low whisper, "I think he's gone."

Chapter 26

Eve was sitting on the exam table in one of the rooms in the emergency department at George Washington University Hospital. The doctor was showing her the x-ray of her foot. As she suspected, the bullet they retrieved was indeed a .22-caliber.

Pointing to the x-ray the doctor said, "You're very fortunate that the bullet was so small. It was slowed slightly by your boot and lodged right here, near the center of the cuboid bone. A larger bullet would have likely shattered this bone, which would have impacted both the fourth and fifth metatarsals here, leading to those toes. Could have also damaged the calcaneus bone right above it here. And then above that, the lateral malleolus, also known as your ankle bone, would have also been impacted. Not to mention all the connecting cartilage. You'd be looking at a long healing, physical therapy and some possible permanent inflexibility."

Eve, who was feeling pretty good, thanks to the shot of Demerol they gave her before extracting the bullet, said, "So it's true." Then, sing-songy, "The toe bone's connected to foot bone, the foot bone's connected to the ankle bone, the ankle bone's connected to leg bone. Dem bones gonna walk around."

Smiling, he said, "Sure, reduce fifteen years of medical education to a spiritual from the 1920's. Why not?"

"Thanks, Doc! Seriously, though. Thank you."

"You're welcome, Ms. Genest. I see this older wound near it, between the second and third metatarsals. What is it about this foot that seems to attract bullets?"

"You know what they say, unlucky in love, lucky in lead."

"Haven't heard that one. How's your pain tolerance?"

"On the high side, I think."

"Then Advil or Tylenol should do the trick. But if you do end up wanting something stronger after the Demerol wears off, just let me know. I'm sending you home with a prescription for Cephalosporin, a single-dose antibiotic. While we cleaned it out very carefully, infections are common with bullet wounds, so get it filled and take it right away."

"Thanks again, Doc."

"Detective Barnes from DC Metro is outside. You feel up to talking to him"

"Sure." Smiling, "I may even sing to him."

A minute after the doctor left, there was a knock on the door.

"Come in."

As he came through the door, Eve thought Detective Barnes looked a lot like Bosch, the main character in Michael Connelly's novels. Actually, like Titus Welliver, the actor who portrayed him in the television series. "How are you feeling, Ms. Genest?"

"You can call me Rose. I'm fine. Be limping for a while. Doc says I'll miss my daily run for a few weeks, but it could have been worse. Compared to the guys I dropped, I'm golden."

"So, tell me what happened."

She did, for the fifth time. Once to the officers who responded to her call. Then to the EMTs who took her to the ER. Then to the hospital admin folks. Then the doctor who treated her. And now the detective.

When she finished, he said, "And you never saw them before?"

"Never," she lied. She wasn't about to tell him they had followed her two weeks earlier and that the Secret Service had identified them. She told him what she told everyone else. That her name was Rose Genest, an artist from Boston who was consulting with the President's Committee on the Arts and Humanities. The Agency even had someone at the Committee's office who would verify Eve's cover if needed.

"Where did you learn to shoot like that?"

"My grandfather taught me. And they were only a few feet away. Hard to miss."

"And you have no idea who these guys were?"

"Not a clue."

"Well, you were quite fortunate, considering. We just identified them. Both known criminals who did prison time. Very dangerous men. Can you think of any reason they would have wanted to harm you?"

"Nope."

In the back of his mind, he couldn't help wondering if the motive was nothing more complex than the commerce of lust. After all, she was movie-star gorgeous. Someone who might be the result if Kristen Bell and Megan Fox could have had a child.

Both perps had prostitution on their rap sheets. Kidnapping and sex slavery were unfortunately all too common—a global plague that left no part of the world untainted. This was the supposition he wrote in his incident report.

She already knew the answer, but asked him anyway, "Why do you think they were using such a small caliber gun?"

"My guess is that if you resisted too hard, they would have shot you. Somewhere nonlethal. Get you to comply without killing you or doing too much damage."

She put on her best shocked face. "I see…"

"It's a good thing you were armed and alert."

"I've had my share of stalkers."

He wasn't surprised and almost said so but instead said, "Sorry to hear that. But good to know you can take care of yourself. Your outcome is not what usually happens in situations like this."

"Thanks. We done?"

"We're done. Hope you heal quickly, Ms. Genest."

"Thanks. According to the doc, dem bones gonna walk around. In a few weeks."

Fortunately, the police had kept the press out of the apartment building's garage, so no pictures of the scene or Eve were taken. The police maintained the standard protocol of not commenting on an ongoing investigation beyond the facts. They stated that two armed men had been killed in a clear case of self-defense. That the woman they attacked was armed. But they did not reveal that she was wounded or her identity for the sake of her privacy and safety.

After she was fitted with a boot cast to immobilize her foot for the next three weeks, she called Leo who picked her up from the ER.

As they drove to her apartment after stopping at the pharmacy, he said, "Two bogies down. Nicely done."

"Not getting shot would have been better."

"What is it about your left foot that seems to attract bullets?"

"The exact question the doctor asked."

"I may start calling you Leadfoot."

"You're *toe*-tally hilarious."

"Seriously, even with a wounded foot, you've just given a serious kick to the hornet's nest. They'll be pissed. So, keep your head on a swivel."

"Always."

After they got to Eve's apartment and Leo made a pot of coffee for her, she shooed him out, convincing him that she was fine.

She then settled on the sofa, turned on the television to see if the news was reporting anything about her incident.

She nearly dropped her coffee cup when a picture of the chief justice came on screen as the news anchor made the breaking announcement of his sudden death, apparently due to a massive heart attack.

She picked up her phone and dialed Marshal Grant. It continued to ring and just as she was preparing to leave a message, he picked up. "Hello, Eve. It's a bit nuts around here, as you can well imagine. Can I call you back tomorrow?"

"Certainly. I just want to say I'm so sorry, Clay."

"Thanks. But it looks like it was a pretty straightforward heart attack. The timing is just awfully coincidental. I was sitting with my partner just outside his chambers when it happened."

"Do you believe in those kinds of coincidences?"

"Not usually."

"When will you be getting the autopsy report?"

"Sometime tomorrow's what I was told."

"If this is what I suspect it is, you'll want to call me."

"That's sounding rather ominous, Eve. What the fuck's going on?"

"When you call me back, I'll share as much as I can with you. But please keep all of this to yourself."

"Okay. Gotta go. Bye."

After ending the call, she opened Leo's app and texted the president, filling him in. She didn't hear back from him. It was very likely he wouldn't even see the text for hours. And she was sure he had already been briefed about Harrison's death.

Since their scheduled biweekly meeting at Jackson Place was tomorrow, she figured he'd most likely wait until then to talk anyway.

She then texted Leo and asked him to let her know as soon as the wiretaps were activated, anticipating that they would be soon.

His text back said, *Shit! But not your fault. All Spinner. Keep on keeping head on a swivel. Will be in touch with any burner activity.*

Chapter 27

Courtney Collins was sitting at the bar with his good friend from the Metro PD, Detective Jack Cooney. Jack also grew up in Ireland, ironically in the next town over from Collins—who was known as Liam Quinn back then. They knew each other, mostly from rugby—they had played on the same regional team when they were in school.

They lost touch when Cooney came to the States with his parents. Cooney's family moved to Baltimore when he was 16 and in the fifth year of his senior school cycle in Ireland, which is the equivalent of a high school junior in the States.

Ten years ago, sitting in this very bar—both drawn to this classic Irish public house named McGinty's by the same heartfelt longing for a taste of home—Jack noticed Courtney's accent and as they struck up a conversation, Jack said Courtney looked familiar. Courtney said the same. At first, Collins was alarmed and guarded, wondering if some of his past had caught up with him. But they quickly discovered who each other was.

Collins told Cooney that he had to change his name, admitting he did so because he had gotten caught up in *The Troubles* back home as a young man. Jack not only understood, but he also said that had his parents not moved away, he would have very likely been at his side.

After high school, Jack attended Georgetown University with a plan to become a lawyer after getting his undergraduate degree. But he fell madly in love with a woman who was also attending Georgetown, and they soon became husband and wife. Their first child, who came a year after their marriage, changed his plans. He then joined the Metro DC police department and quickly rose through the ranks to become a detective.

Not wanting to reveal the true nature of his work and his criminal past, Collins told Jack that he was a sales consultant for a weapons manufacturer and that negotiating business deals with governments and their militaries brought him all over the globe. It was a lie that was just close enough to the truth to give credence to Courtney's occasional requests for help from his good friend, including the recent use of traffic cameras to locate Eve.

Collins told Jack that the nature of his business drew a lot of corporate espionage from other gun manufacturers and the countless number of DC gun lobbyists who worked for them. He told Jack that Eve was one of these lobbyists and that he needed to keep tabs on her because of a large contract with Canada that he was in the middle of negotiating. Said his competition was known to resort to espionage and even outright theft to gain any inside information about the deal. So, he asked Jack for his help. Of course, he was willing and none the wiser.

Why would he be?

They had become as close as brothers over the years. Often coming to each other's houses for the holidays. They attended each family's big events—birthdays and graduations. That was until Collins' wife passed away three years ago from breast cancer. Their only son, Liam, was now living with his girlfriend in Cupertino, California, working as a software engineer for Apple.

As Courtney and Jack were drinking their Guinness, mugshot images of Vincent Gianni and Frank Bateau came onto the flat-screen TV that hung above the bar directly in front of them. Courtney nearly choked on his beer mid sip. Jack said, "What's wrong? You look like you've seen a ghost."

He composed himself as best and quickly as he could. "Nothing really. One of those guys looked familiar, that's all."

"I doubt you knew those fuckers. Hell's Angels. Both of 'em. One from New York, the other from Quebec. They were shot in the garage of the Woodward. Hey, that's the same apartment we traced that woman to, isn't it? What are the odds?"

"What are the odds, indeed?"

"The detective who caught the case, Barnes, said a woman took 'em out. She did catch a bullet in the foot. Small caliber. A clear case of self-defense. Shot each of them twice. Heart and head. Close range. Hollow points. Big mess.

"Barnes said she was absolutely gorgeous. So, his working theory is that these guys, who both did time for prostitution, among a long and sordid list of other federal offenses in the States and Canada, were attempting to kidnap her, sell her into sex slavery."

"Sex slavery? Really?"

"Happens all the time."

"Fucked up world, ain't it?"

"You have no idea, my friend. I spend the first half of most nights trying to forget the shit I've seen. Fucked up world doesn't even come close."

"You look ready for another," Courtney said as he gestured to the bartender to draw two more pints from the tap. They then ordered from the menu, a mix of traditional Irish fare and typical pub food. Jack ordered the Shepherd's Pie and Courtney the Beef and Guinness Stew. *When in Rome. Or an Irish pub.*

They ate as they watched a futból match—they will never, ever call it soccer—between the U.S. men's national team and Slovenia. But while Courtney's eyes were on the screen, his mind was ten thousand miles away—the distance from DC to Australia.

After the match had ended and one more Guinness, it was Courtney's turn to pick up the tab. They said their goodbyes with an affirmation to do it again in two weeks.

Twenty minutes later, when Courtney was back in his living room, he took the burner phone from an end-table drawer, called Robin, and left a short message.

He then sat back in his chair, put his feet up on the coffee table and picked up where he left off, once again lost in deep thought.

He was already close to solidifying Plan B.

Chapter 28

Eve and President Olson were in the Oval Office going over the events of the last three days. With his vice president on the other side of the globe, not to mention that she already knew Eve was involved, he wanted to hold their regular meeting in the Oval today. It also meant the president would be able to spend a bit more time with her and personally thank her for taking a bullet for him.

They were sitting across from each other on the chairs facing the fireplace—Eve's leg was propped up on a footstool—when her phone rang. It was Deputy Marshal Grant.

Eve had spent some time over the last couple of days looking into Clay's background. He had been with the Judicial Security Division of the U.S. Marshals Service as a Deputy for the last decade, so he had Top Security clearance. Graduated near the top of his class from Glynco. Assigned to lead the chief justice's security detail three years ago. Prior to becoming a Marshal, he had served in the Navy as a SEAL for ten years, some of that time, she noted, was in Afghanistan, around the same time she served.

While all this appealed to her, she was most impressed by the fact that for the first six years he was working as a Marshal, he attended George Washington University at night and earned a degree in psychology.

She admittedly perked up when she saw he had never been married. At first, it concerned her, but she realized their paths were quite similar and they were likely single for many of the same reasons. She wanted to know more. And she could tell he did, too.

She looked from her phone to the president and said "I was expecting this call, and I'd like to put it on speaker if that's okay with you, Mr. President. It's the Marshal I mentioned."

"Certainly. Go ahead."

Eve answered, "Hello, Clay."

"Hi, Eve. Got the autopsy report."

"Let me guess, he was poisoned."

"Yup. What's going on?"

"I'm with someone here who can answer that. Go ahead, Mr. President."

"Are you seri— "

"Good afternoon, Deputy Marshall Grant."

"Holy shit! Oh, geez, sorry, Mr. President."

"No worries. Holy shit, indeed. The autopsy found a lethal mix of digoxin and fentanyl, didn't it?"

"Exactly. Did you also get the report, sir?"

"No. The same combination killed Senator Trahison a year ago. The same person is behind Justice Harrison's death. I've already put a lid on this autopsy report. The real cause of death won't be released to the public just yet. As far as the world knows, for the time being, Justice Harrison had a fatal heart attack. Only you and a few others know the truth. I can't get into the details of all this any further, Deputy Marshal. And I need you to keep it all to yourself. Can you do that for me?"

"Absolutely, sir."

"Good man. And I want you to do something else for me."

"Anything, Mr. President."

"Support Eve in any way she asks."

"Yes, sir."

"And treat her well, Mr. Grant. This is one very special woman. She's like a daughter to me."

Eve said, "Oh, Mr. President, that's awfully sweet."

"I mean it, Eve."

Grant said, "Yes, sir. While she and I have only known each other briefly, something I hope to change as soon as possible, I want to say something that I've always wanted to—I serve at the pleasure of the President of the United States."

"I appreciate that, son." He chuckled a bit. "But in this case, it would be better if you served at the pleasure of Eve Tuant."

"Yes, sir."

Eve said, I'll call you later, Clay."

"Talk to you then. And thank you, Mr. President." Eve ended the call.

The president said, "He seems sincere. But is he cute?"

Eve laughed. "Very."

"I trust he won't catch any flack for the justice's death."

"I'm not sure, sir. I'm guessing he may be looking at some questions internally about the timing of Harrison's security threat increase and his demise. But it's hard to say what kind of pressure he'll face."

"I'll put a subtle word into the Justice Department. That should help."

"Perfect, sir. One of the justice's law clerks mentioned an old man handing him two packets of brown sugar when he and the others were in Starbucks. Since the sugar is the source of the poison, I've got Leo looking at their security camera footage. Heading to Langley once you and I are done, sir. I'll let you know what we find."

He replied, "I read the clerk interviews. They said that the Chief Justice's last words were, *fucking spin*. They thought perhaps he was dizzy. But you and I know that he meant Spinner. He knew she had killed him. Just couldn't finish saying her name."

"You read the transcript, sir. The justice was extremely rattled by my coming to his house. He even threatened the VP."

"Fatal mistake on his part."

"Indeed, sir. He underestimated her. Or he believed that due to his position she'd never dare do him any harm. The same thought crossed my mind as well. I didn't think she'd kill him. And he knew how Trahison died… I can't help but feel some responsibility, Mr. President."

"One of the things I admire about you, Eve, is your balance. Extraordinarily lethal competence and deep, heartfelt empathy. It's rare. Most lean one way or the other. If it helps, accept the fact that you did it for me. When Truman held this office, he famously said, *the buck stops here*. Well, sometimes it starts here.

"As your Commander in Chief, I want you to know you not only did the right thing, but you also need to understand that you're empowered to do it again. And as your friend, I'm extremely grateful for everything, Eve. For all the sacrifices you're making." Pointing to her foot, "How's it healing?"

"I'll probably be able to predict the weather in a few years, but it seems to be healing well. Hurts less even after a few days. I'm already putting more weight on it."

"You've got me wondering if we shouldn't look into developing bullet-proof shoes."

"Like the sound of that. I could use a new pair of Manolo Blahniks. Got something in blue satin?"

Chapter 29

After leaving the White House at 9:30 a.m., Eve had to struggle through dense downtown congestion. As she did, she checked her rear-view mirrors frequently, *head on a swivel*, finally making her way to Langley over an hour later.

Leo was showing her what he found on the Starbucks security footage. He said, "Coverage isn't great. The store, like most in retail, is mostly concerned with what goes on with the cash register. But there is this." He fast-forwarded the footage to an elderly man walking into the shop. In the background, his image was distorted by the bend of the wide-angle lens. Then he went to the register to order, where he came into a clearer but still somewhat bowed view. Eve said, "He *does* look like Bernie Sanders."

He purchased his coffee, turned, walked over and stood in front of the kiosk holding the items people add to coffee—as well as stirrers, cardboard cup sleeves, and paper napkins—trying to look busy. Leo said, "Here are the Chief Justice's law clerks. It took watching this several times to see it but keep your eyes on the old guy. I'll slow it down. There." Eve said, "He's putting sugar packets into his pocket."

Leo said, "Now, Jason Nevells, the clerk who said he looked like Bernie Sanders, comes over and sees the empty brown sugar bin and says something. The old guy holds up two packets and offers them to Jason, who takes them, and they exchange a few words. After a minute the old man follows them out the door and all we can see is legs and torsos—the kids turning left heading to the Court and he goes north toward Maryland Avenue."

Eve asked, "Are there any traffic cameras on Maryland Ave?"

"Just some red-light cams at the intersection of Second, Constitution, and Maryland. I checked them. Nothing."

"We should have enough to run facial scans, yes?"

"That's what I've been working on most this morning. I've taken what we got from Starbucks and run it through three different AI image-generating apps. Have a couple headshots here. And something that's gonna blow your mind."

Pointing, Eve said, "This one looks closest, does it?"

"That's the one I've been working with. I took the image and wrote prompts that removed all the aging features—hair, eyebrows, wrinkles, jowls, wattle, etcetera. Watch this." He hit the return key.

"Holy shit," Eve said. "That's Courtney Collins."

"An AI version of him, but yes. Not sure it will hold up in court."

"We won't be going to court, Leo. You know that."

"I do. Just—" Leo's monitor interrupted him with a repetitive ping.

Eve said, "What was that?"

As he clicked the mouse over an icon, "Wiretap's active. Let's listen."

CC: "Hello, Madame Vice President."

RS: "I've got some downtime before we fly back to DC. Saw the news. Nice work. Any loose ends?"

CC: "None. Went perfectly."

RS: "I saw the autopsy report, and it concluded heart attack."

Eve looked at Leo and said, "The president didn't say anything to me, but she got fed the same fake report that was released to the public. Smart man. Glad I voted for him."

CC: "Good to know. The chemistry's always tricky. Part science, part art."

RS: "You've got Tuant now, yes?"

CC: "No. She sent my guys to the morgue."

RS: "Fuck! Now she'll be hypervigilant. Damn it, Courtney! You said these were pros."

CC: "They were. I did some more diggin.' Seems our girl has a shit-ton of combat experience. You told me she was in the Canadian army. Afghanistan vet. But you never mentioned she was special forces."

RS: "I didn't know. I told you, she's CIA. Their files are impervious. God himself needs permission to access. How'd you find out?"

CC: "I know people, who know people, who know."

RS: "What now? I still need answers."

CC: "I up the ante. She's got family in Quebec. Grandparents. Easy snatch and grab. She'll answer all your questions then."

Eve didn't listen to the rest. She immediately took her cell to the next cubicle and called her grandfather. She then made another call.

RS: "Make it happen."

CC: "Already on it. One of the guys she killed is from there. The other was a friend of his from New York who lived in Quebec with his girl. So, the four friends of theirs I'm sendin' will be highly motivated."

RS: "Don't screw it up."

CC: "Good as done."

RS: Gotta go. Heading to the airport. I'll be back in DC tomorrow. Keep me posted."

"CC: Got it. Talk later."

Eve returned to Leo's cubicle after a few minutes. "What'd I miss?"

"Looks like he's sending some more Quebec Hell's Angels. Will your grandparents be okay?"

She looked at the transcript for the last bit of the conversation she missed. "He doesn't know it yet, but Courtney just ordered four more body bags."

Chapter 30

The farmhouse that Eve grew up in was built in 1675 by her grandfather's ancestor, whose son enlarged it in 1710. The Tuants were a settler family. Eve's great-grandfather-times-twelve, Henry, came from France to Quebec in 1635. He settled on the Île d'Orléans, an island in the St. Lawrence River that's located three miles east of Quebec City. Henry was a soldier who left the army three years after arriving to settle and trap and trade furs.

He became so successful, a decade later he petitioned the young King Louis XIV in a letter he sent along with two-thousand furs for half of the island's 48,000 total acres, which the King granted, making Henry Tuant one of New France's first Seigneurs.

While Henry knew that France could certainly lay claim to land and call it New France, he understood that it also belonged to the people who had lived, built, hunted, trapped, and fished on it for millennia.

He had grown close to many of the tribes and clans in the region that he trapped and traded with, including the Abenaki, Algonquin, Cree and Mi'kmaq. But especially the Huron-Wendat or "dwellers of the island" who lived nearby.

He was not only fur-trading partners with this Huron tribe, but he also treated them as equals and learned their language. However, the primary reason his Native partners considered him one of their own and adopted him as a member of their tribe, occurred during the Beaver Wars.

Henry fought alongside the Wyandot against the Mohawks during several skirmishes on the Isle, when Mohawk war parties traversed the St. Lawrence River to attack French settlements and the villages of other tribes.

During one of these fierce battles, Henry saved the Wyandot chief's son's life, shooting a Mohawk warrior in the head just as he was about to strike the young man from behind with a war club. When he ran out of ammunition shortly thereafter, Henry dashed headlong into the battle, his tomahawk in one hand and the war club dropped by the warrior he shot in the other. He struck down twelve more Mohawk before the battle was over, and a handful of the remaining Mohawk war party barely escaped in their canoes.

During their victory celebration that night, the Wyandot chief gave Henry the name, *Fierce White Bear.* He also gave Henry his daughter's hand in marriage. Which was the reason Eve's DNA was ninety-five percent French and five-percent Huron.

While the Beaver Wars ended ten years before Henry started building his house, his firsthand experiences witnessing the unspeakable brutality of the Mohawks, not to mention the harsh Canadian winters, were the reasons Henry built the now three-thousand-square-foot house completely out of fieldstone. The walls, painted white throughout the interior of the house, are three-feet thick—built to stop bullets and even small cannon fire.

Needless to say, the farmhouse was built to last. Every hand-hewn beam and nearly every pinewood floorboard were still solidly in place three-hundred and fifty years later. The house had been lovingly cared for and updated by generations of Tuants.

While much of the original land had been sold off over the

years, almost all of it to farmers looking to cultivate the rich, diverse, hilly island soil, the family still owned twenty acres, as well as the Île Madame, a small island that sits in the St. Lawrence River a mile and half south of Orleans' northwest tip. It's just shy of 4-miles long and a mile at its widest point, and only accessible by boat or small plane. The family leases half of it to a commercial fishing company.

Eve was three years-old when she came to live with her grandparents after her parents died. Her father, Henry Jr., the eldest of her grandparents' four sons, and her mother, Olivia, were killed in a plane crash.

Eve's dad wanted to combine a business trip with their fourth wedding anniversary. Henry needed to go to Gary, Indiana, to Gary Works, the largest steel manufacturing plant in the U.S., located on the south shore of Lake Michigan. He went to tour the facilities and sign a contract for 150,000 pounds of a special steel alloy he needed for three tugboats his company was just commissioned to build for the Port of Virginia.

On the morning of February 13th, Eve's parents boarded the corporate jet and flew out of Quebec City, landing at the Gary/Chicago Airport two hours later. The plan was that once his business meeting was completed, Henry and his lovely wife were to then fly to New York City for a weekend anniversary celebration.

But after taking off from Gary later that afternoon, the plane, a Challenger 600, suffered catastrophic failure of both engines and control of all ailerons, flaps, and elevators five minutes into the flight, causing the jet to plummet seventeen-thousand feet into icy Lake Michigan.

Eve's three uncles—Jacques, four years younger than her father, Guy, seven years younger, and Bertrand, ten years

younger—immediately took to Eve. They were enthralled to
have a little sister. They loved her deeply, and while they tried
to treat her like a princess, she would have none of it.

She played hockey, baseball and soccer with them. She
fished the St. Lawrence River, hunted deer in Northern Quebec,
and went canoeing, hiking and rock climbing with them. She
stood shoulder-to-shoulder with them cheering on the Montreal
Canadians as they took the ice at the Molson Centre.

Her grandparents filled the hole of her missing mom and dad
as best they could. Eve flourished as a result. She loved spending
time with her grandmother every day after school, cultivating
the greenhouse, learning the rhythms of seasonal vegetables,
fruits, herbs, and flowers and how to tend to them. She learned
how to bake bread in the oven that was built into one side of
the home's enormous fireplace more than three centuries earlier.
And she mastered her grandmother's recipe for Tourtière, which
she made every Christmas and New Year's Eve.

Whenever he could, her grandfather took Eve with him nearly
everywhere he went, including the company shipyard where she
learned about block-assembly methods, crane capacity, manual
and automatic welding techniques, CAD drawings, production
planning and budgeting. She watched tankers, bulk carriers,
tugboats, container ships, Canadian Navy destroyers, cruisers
and frigates being built, converted, and repaired.

And she often served as his assistant as he turned steel and
iron into amazing objects of art in the property's barn that he
had converted into a studio.

There was simply no way on earth Eve would allow a single
hair on the heads of her family to be harmed. Or even a single
pinecone on the property to be crushed.

Not by anyone. Ever.

Two SUVs carrying four Hell's Angels from Quebec City crossed the St. Lawrence River at the Pont de l'Île bridge. Once on the Île d'Orléans, they took a left onto Chemin Royale Road, also known as Route 368. They drove east for twelve miles, then took a right onto Chemin de la Butte. As they began to climb the steep-hilled road leading through the Tuant property to the farmhouse at the top of the butte, a motion sensor that lay buried in the road several yards into their climb sent an alert to a cell phone.

The two cars made their way through the open iron gate attached to two twelve-foot fieldstone pillars and followed the driveway toward the house. They parked next to the walkway that wound through the gardened yard leading to the red front door framed and surrounded by walls of gray granite fieldstones. Four men, two from each car, climbed out. Each was dressed in blue jeans, motorcycle boots and sleeveless leather vests with large Hell's Angels patches on their backs—the ubiquitous Angel's uniform.

Peter Beauvoir, Al Renault, and Stephen Lisle, were carrying AR-15s. Guy Sourette, the leader, had a Glock 19 in his hand. Guy waved it at Beauvoir and Lisle indicating that they should go around to the back of the house. He and Renault headed toward the front door, following the curved fieldstone path.

He rapped on the front door with his gun. "Mister and Missus Tuent. Open up. We need to talk to you."

From inside, Eve's grandfather, Henry, loudly said, "If you want to continue to live you should leave right now." Guy and Al looked at each other and laughed, then Guy said, "Get the fuck out here now or we'll fill your house with holes."

Henry said, "Will you also huff and puff? You were warned. It's your funeral, assholes!"

Guy signaled for Al to begin firing into the door and windows when the ground around them erupted and sprung to life. Two soldiers in ghillie suits that had blended seamlessly and invisibly into the garden around them stood, one on each side at a forty-five-degree angle, only four feet away, their MP5s pointed directly at the two men. At the same moment, in the back of the house, two other soldiers did the same to Beauvoir and Lisle.

Guy stiffened, then snarled, "Fuck you!" as he lifted his gun. He never got it higher than a foot before short bursts from both MP5s put twenty 9-millimeter rounds into his body. Seeing his long-time friend fall, Al turned and started to lift his AR-15 and instantly met the same bullet-riddled fate.

Hearing the shots at the front of the house, Beauvoir and Lisle reacted the same way and were also cut down where they stood.

After hearing Courtney's plan to kidnap her grandparents, the second phone call Eve had made from Leo's office was to a member of her former Joint Task Force 2 team, Lieutenant Jason LaBeauf. He then called and mobilized three other JFT2 team members who dropped what they were doing and came locked and loaded to the Tuant's home that same day.

They spent a day and a half with the Tuants as their guests and laid the groundwork to greet their unwelcome visitors once they arrived.

Every member of Eve's Afghanistan special ops team, Canadians and Americans alike, would lay their lives down for her without blinking.

And each one knew she would do the same for them.

Chapter 31

Courtney Collins was grilling a small steak on his back patio when his cell rang. Noting the caller, he answered, putting it on speaker while he turned over a potato wrapped in foil and said, "It's about time. Been waitin' for your call. You got em?"

"Just left the fucking morgue. The Sûreté du Québec came to the clubhouse this morning. Needed someone to identify the bodies of my guys. They were all riddled with fucking bullet holes! The cops then spent the next four hours sweating me for details. So no, I don't fucking got em' and I'm not gonna fucking get em'!"

Courtney took the phone off speaker and held it to his ear, his voice rising with each sentence. "You mean to tell me your guys couldn't pick up a 70-something-year-old couple? That a pair of white-haired grandparents got the drop on four Angels? Are you fuckin' shittin' me? You runnin' a motorcycle gang or a fuckin' knitting circle? Did the guys you sent pull themselves away from makin' doilies and knitting sweaters?"

"Fuck you, asshole! One word from me and your life is over, motherfucker!"

Gritting his teeth, straining to calm his voice, something he had become very practiced at doing after so many years of dealing with hotheaded, thin-skinned warlords, gangsters, and militia all over the globe, Courtney said, "Look, we've been workin' together for a long time. No point in makin' threats. You know damn well that cuts both ways, Harry. Just tell me what the fuck went down."

"The cops were sketchy with details. Said that the old man had security. Seems he does business with the Navy. Did you know he owns the fifth-largest shipbuilding business in Canada?"

"No. Didn't really look into the grandparents. All I know is the old man's an artist. A sculptor. She's a housewife. Figured it was a simple snatch and grab."

"Well, you figured wrong. Big fucking time. And I'm serious. You and I are done. I've lost six guys. Not losing any more. And the cops said that because of the Navy connection, now the fucking CSIS will be all over our asses. You're bad for business, Collins. Don't fuckin' call me again." The line went dead.

Courtney's steak had burnt to a crisp. He picked it up and screamed, "Fuck!" as he hurled it over the fence and into the trees in his backyard.

He was not looking forward to the next call he had to make.

But first he needed to work out Plan C.

Chapter 32

Eve and Clay were sitting in the Capital Grille, at a small table in a corner by an inwardly curved wall of floor-to-ceiling frosted windows. They were surrounded by walls and ceilings of dark, rich wood panels and coffered beams that gave the restaurant a warm yet commanding vibe. The kind of place where a billion-dollar business deal could be made at one table and an intimate marriage proposal at another.

They had just received their drinks. Eve was having a Blackberry Bourbon Sidecar, which contained Angel's Envy Bourbon, Cointreau, blackberries, fresh lemon juice and thyme. Clay ordered the Capital Grill's famous, Stoli Doli, which is Stoli vodka infused with fresh Dole pineapple, chilled, and served straight up.

Eve said, "Love the two bison heads over the bar."

"You mean Mike and Ike?"

"Their names are Mike and Ike? Cute."

"Did you know that both male and female bison have horns?"

"No, I didn't. If that's so, then how do they know if Mike and Ike aren't actually Michelle and Irene?"

"Good point. Not sure."

Smiling at him, "Well, I guess it really only matters that the bison can tell the difference."

After placing their food orders—both were having the lobster bisque to start and the filet mignon, medium rare. She was having hers with the parmesan truffle fries and grilled asparagus with lemon mosto and he was also having the asparagus but with Sam's mashed potatoes.

Clay took a sip of his drink and said, "I must say I've never been ordered by the President of the United States to be nice to a date before. Adds a whole new level of first-date anxiety."

Eve said, "No pressure. You heard him. All you have to do is serve at the pleasure of Eve Tuant."

"How am I doing so far?"

Taking a sip of her drink, she said, "Oh, my, that's tasty.' Looking deeply into his eyes. "So far, Eve Tuant is quite pleased."

He held her gaze. "Good. I'll have you complete my survey at the end of the evening in hopes of achieving five stars… Look, I know you and POTUS mentioned that there's a lid on what's going on, but is there anything you *can* tell me?"

"I can tell you that this is all connected to the Greater Boston Massacre."

"Really? Shit. You were involved in that?"

"Heavily. Look, before I get into it, I must ask two things."

"Name 'em."

"First, is your Top-Secret clearance still in effect?"

"Absolutely. Can't work in Judicial Security without it. Second question?"

"Do you swear to keep anything we discuss to yourself? Most of what I'll tell you is now public knowledge, but some is not."

"Look, I was serious when I said I serve at the President's pleasure. I actually applied for a Secret Service position a month ago. This is more than a job to me." Leaning toward her. "So, yes, I'll take whatever we talk about to the grave if you want me to, Eve." She felt a shiver. The intensity of his demeanor and the timbre of his deep voice sent a tremor through her entire body. She paused to regroup, looked at her drink for a moment before diving back into his deep green-eyed pool.

"Thank you, Clay. Where to begin. I actually live in Boston. Been in DC for the last few months. Moving back once all this business is finished." She noticed a flinch of pain in his eyes when she said that. "I lead the Homeland team that you heard and read about. My name has been intentionally kept out of it. So far, at least."

After some of his drink, "Were you at the lighthouse?"

"Yes. I'm the one who took out Trahison."

"I'm not surprised."

"No? How come?"

"It makes sense. Why else would you be working on it here, with the president, if not to finish what you'd started. And the Chief Justice was obviously part of the cabal."

Eve swirled the blackberries in her drink and then a big sip. "How observant of you. Add a star to the survey. Yes, he was. There's one more member and someone working with that person. At least that we know of. If there are other players in this, they've remained hidden. But we're getting close to wrapping these two up in a nice, evidence-laced bow."

"Whatever I can do to help, say the word."

"I appreciate that. I'm just sorry you lost your protectee."

"I'm still in court for oral arguments as usual. And I'll now rotate with my team members on the other eight justices' residences. At least until the president names the next chief justice."

"Did you catch any flack over his death?"

"Oddly enough, no. I expected to get some heat over recently increasing his threat level coverage and then losing him shortly thereafter, but it's been quiet. After our phone call, I suspect the president may have had something to do with that."

"You're batting a thousand so far, Clay. Keep it up."

A smoky voice and sly grin, "I intend to." She held his eyes, smiled and felt a bit of a blush hit her cheeks. She was picturing him naked. Again.

The waiter arrived with their food and placed it in front of them. They both said yes to another drink, and he brought those while they started eating. They thanked him and he slipped away as if on cue, like any good waiter who can read his customer's vibes.

After they had been eating for a while, Eve asked, "You were a SEAL?"

In between chews, "For a decade or so. You were with JTF2 weren't you? Impressive group. We teamed up with a few in 'Stan. SEAL brass bragged about you guys."

"You've done your homework."

Wiping his mouth with a napkin, "So have you. How many women have made that elite group?"

Covering her mouth full of food with her hand, "So far, just me."

"Wow. I'm impressed. Women have yet to break the SEAL barrier. Although I believe it's only a matter of time."

"How do you feel about that?"

He placed his knife and fork onto his nearly empty plate. "I'm all for it. And I'm not just saying that because I'm sitting here with you." After a sip of his drink, "I've got three sisters, and any one of them could kick the asses of many of the guys I served with on the Teams. I'm not a gender snob. If you can do the job, it doesn't matter to me whether you've got breasts or not."

"I call them chesticles."

Clay was sipping his drink and nearly sprayed it across the table as he laughed. He put his napkin to his mouth and took a moment to recover. "Chesticles. That'll be my next text to my sisters. For sure."

Eve said, "It looks like we were in 'Stan around the same time. Where were you?"

"Early in the conflict I led some ODAs in the mountains," he answered referring to Operational Detachment Alphas. "We broke into several three- or four-man teams so that we could cover more terrain. Two or three SEALs with at least one Afghan militia who knew the area intimately. We were trained to direct tactical airstrikes, using targeting lasers and satellite-linked global positioning devices to guide smart bombs onto targets."

"I've used those satellite dishes a few times. Look like spider webs on short stands on the ground."

"They kinda do, don't they? Small, light, easy to set up anywhere. Woulda been lost without 'em. We worked in shifts. Kept the bombs falling on the Taliban round the clock. First on their battle trenches and encampments and then we tracked them to their caves."

Eve said, "Warheads on foreheads."

"Exactly. What about you? Where?"

"Cities mostly. Kabul and then Kandahar. Identifying and targeting Taliban command nodes. Intelligence gathering. Snatch and grab ops. Led some very high-level scores. Which is what got the CIA's attention, and they recruited me. What do you miss most about your time in 'Stan?"

"I know it sounds nuts, but I miss my sheep's wool Pakol hat."

"Seriously? I always thought the guys looked like they were wearing a pie in a pie plate on their head."

"With those and our beards, we not only blended in with the natives, our heads were also warm and weatherproof. You know what the weather can be like over there. Fashion takes a back seat to warm and dry any day. It's in the eye of the beholder anyway. For all we know, a nice Pakol gets Afghan women all hot and bothered."

"Sure. They may like their guys with pies. And I could see you with a beard. I like this look better. But I could see it. What about later in the war?"

"Mostly raids on Taliban compounds. We owned the skies, as you know, so drones and aircraft were free to roam and locate."

"Any ops in particular stand out?"

"Quite a few actually. But one of my last sticks out most. I prefer dwelling on memories of the ops that went well instead of those that didn't. Replay them in my head."

"I do that, too. The ones that went wrong also get airtime. Hard not to. But I try to switch to the ones that went right. And sometimes they even show up in my dreams," Eve said.

Their dessert and coffee arrived. Both had ordered Crème Brulé and as Eve moved a few berries sitting on top out of the way with her spoon and broke the sugar crust, she said, "So, the op. Spill deets."

"There was a compound in Kunar that we scoped out. High-altitude drones found it. Our usual protocol was straight forward. Kill Taliban fighters and conduct SSE (Sensitive Information Evaluation). Our plan was to infiltrate through some mountain terrain that the Taliban considered impassible. But we needed to get in undetected. If they knew we were coming, it would have been a suicide mission. There were way too many places to be ambushed. Too much enemy high ground.

"We knew the Taliban had lookouts everywhere, especially

around our bases. So, my team left the base with a large formation of Army regulars. We'd all travel together for some distance and then my team would break off and sneak away unseen, while the regulars would continue on as distraction bait."

"Smart move. Whose idea was that?"

"Mine."

"Ooo. Chalk up another survey star."

He smiled. "So, we were able to use their own route of mountain trails and passages to get to the target compound. It was nearly unnavigable. Why they picked the location. They figured we'd never find it, and we'd certainly never come in that way. They were wrong. And they never knew what hit 'em.

"We had suppressors on our HK416s, on a couple of M249s and on the TAC338 sniper rifle. Took out all twenty-two Taliban fighters with surgical precision. Fish in a pond. Not a single SEAL casualty. Although one member of my team, Albertson, badly sprained his ankle. We all gave him a really hard time. Asked if he wanted to be evacced or would he like us to find him a baby carriage. When we got back to base, Reynolds, one of my snipers, made and presented him with a black-and-blue heart... Anyway, we went in and found lots of intelligence. Two laptops. Some cell phones. Destroyed their sizable stash of weapons and ammo on our way out."

"Wait, was this August of '12?"

"It was, yes. Why?"

"Talk about incredibly coincidental. That intel came to me."

"Seriously? What are the odds?"

"I can't do that kind of math. One of the laptops you found included three scheduled resupplies. Dates and locations. Our team got set up for each with some laser targeting designators. Had a pair of A-10s greet them. We cleaned up the leftovers.

Took out tons of ammo, food, all their trucks and a whole bunch of Taliban to boot. Thanks to you."

"Thanks to my team."

"Wow. Survey stars keep adding up… Okay, now the most important question of the evening."

"Uh-oh. Sounds serious."

"Why aren't you married?"

"Same reasons I assume you're not. Away a lot. And when you're home, you can be moody because of what you saw and did, but unable to talk about it. Not only for security, but because they simply won't get it. Not their fault. They just have no reference. No context. Like you're speaking a foreign language.

"It makes for rather acidic relational fodder. And it all adds up to short-term connections. At best. Same for you?"

"Frighteningly so. With an up on the ante. The last guy I was in love with shot me in the foot. And planned to kill me." She slid her booted foot out from under the table and said, "Same foot, by the way."

"What?"

"He was with me at the lighthouse."

"Oh, shit. Hunter-something. Homeland."

"Forte. Hunter Forte."

"Poisoned the senator. Executed his chief of staff. That guy?"

"That guy. We were together for more than a year. Had no clue he was part of the cabal until the president told me. Showed me evidence just before we went to the lighthouse."

"Holy shit. I'd swear off relationships forever after that."

"I thought I had." Meeting his unwavering gaze. "Fate had other plans. Or, as a very close friend of mine would say, God had other plans. Or so it would seem. A bit early to tell."

"I certainly don't want to make you feel uncomfortable, Eve.

No pressure. I've never met *anyone* like you before. So, I'm fine with taking things as slow as you like. I know it's early, but this feels like something special. Something worth waiting for. We can even go glacial. Your call."

"You just got another survey star."

"How many are left?"

"Just one. We'll go to my place after this. See if you can earn it."

Chapter 33

Eve was in the Woodward's gym, which was on the apartment building's ground floor, working on her second set of curls—her eyes on the wall of mirrors checking her form as she lifted and counted reps.

A noticeable grin kept forming across her lips as she continued replaying last night with Clay. It was everything she imagined it would be and then some. He was a passionate, eager, yet gentle lover who saw to her desires over his own. And that made her hunger for him even more. He even made her feel good about the pronounced two-inch-wide scar that runs from between her breasts all the way to her pubic bone. He said it was the highway between her well-crowned mountains to her lush, hidden valley—a highway that he traversed intimately. And often. It was a night so intoxicating and utterly fulfilling that it seemed to have erased all others from her memory.

It made her feel so good about herself, she was doing something she hadn't done in a very long time. She was in a public place exposing her glorious scar for the world to see. Viewing it through Clay's eyes—not as a flaw, but a part of who she was. While she already believed this to be true of herself, no one had confirmed her feelings like this before. She felt content. Blissful. Whole. Scars and all.

The Supreme Court was in session this morning, so Clay had to leave early to get home, shower, change and arrive an hour before the first of two oral arguments started at 10:00 a.m. The Court typically hears two cases when they're in session, and he told her he's usually done an hour after the second session ends.

So, they had agreed to meet at Grazie Nonna at 7:00, an Italian restaurant located just three blocks north of her apartment. The late August weather would be perfect this evening, so they booked a table on their spacious outdoor patio.

She was looking forward to it. Her mind was wandering vividly and wantonly to after-dinner activities back at her place when the phone in her thigh pocket started vibrating. Sliding it out, noting the caller, "Hey, Leo! What's up with you this fine morning?"

"My, my, someone's awfully chipper. Let me guess. Things are going well with your Marshal."

She answered with a sing-songy, "But I did not shoot the deputy."

"Oh, boy. Never heard you sing before. I don't think I've even heard you hum. You've got it bad."

"So bad. But I'm sure that's not why you called. What's up?"

"Got a bead on Courtney. Know where he lives. Quite the tony estate in Chevy Chase. I'll text you his address."

"Traffic cams picked him up?"

"They did. But we didn't really need them to. Turns out, unlike all the others, he leaves his burner on. Didn't check for this since it totally breaks with the pattern."

"Good. Much easier to follow loaves than breadcrumbs."

"Indeed. Also got a transcript from his last wiretap. Seems our guys scared the hell out of the Hell's Angels. No real surprise. You said you called LaBeauf, so who else went with him?"

"He called Boudreau, Ellis, and Fournier."

"Oh, shit, he called the A-Team. Ghillie suits and all?"

She reached into the boot cast to scratch a maddening itch. "Yes. Hidden in plain sight. One of the Angels nearly stepped on Fournier on his way to the front door."

"Well, it worked. Some guy named Harry, the leader it seems, was quite pissed."

"Harry Auclair. Quebec's Hell's Angels president for quite a few years now."

"Seems CSIS is now all over his ass because your grandfather does business with the Navy."

"Ouch. The last thing any criminal in Canada wants is to be on the Canadian Security Intelligence Service's radar. Canada's version of the CIA. They're relentless. But fuck Harry and his minions. Got what they deserved."

As she said this a woman in workout garb entered the gym. Up to this point, she'd had the place to herself.

"That explains why he's freaking out. Even threatened Courtney's life. Anyway, it will make for a fun listen and read when you're here next."

"Be by around lunchtime. I'll bring bacon cheeseburgers from Ebbitt's."

"Ooo. Add caramelized onions to mine, please."

"Done. See you then."

"Bye."

The woman who had arrived started working on the lat pull-down machine with her back to Eve. She appeared to be about the same age as Eve, a bit taller with long red hair that Eve could tell was natural and it framed her pale, freckled face. Another woman, also wearing leggings and a sport bra entered the room. She was carrying a cloth bag with leather handles that she placed next to her as she went over to the nearby rack of kettlebells and picked up two five-pounders.

As Eve headed over to the rowing machine on the other side of the room, the woman at the lat machine said, "Excuse me, I hate to bother ya in the middle of your routine, but could ya please help me with this? Can't seem to get this pin outta the plates."

Eve noted the Irish accent as she replied, "Certainly." She stepped over to the machine and the woman said, "Thanks so much. Name's Grace. I just moved in."

"Nice to meet you, Grace. I'm Rose." As Eve came beside her and reached for the pin that was attached to the stack of weight plates, two things struck her at once. The first was the unease she felt when she heard Grace's Irish brogue, the second was 50,000 volts delivered by the TASER X26 gun, set on drive-stun mode, that the second woman applied directly to the right side of Eve's neck. Usually, the X26 is fired like a pistol from a distance, and two wired electrodes pierce the skin to deliver the debilitating shock. But it's even more effective when applied directly.

The pain was instantaneous and unrelenting. Vibrating fire coursed through her entire body as every muscle clenched like a vice, pulsated and gyrated as she dropped like a rock. Grace caught her and placed her onto the floor. Her brain felt like M&Ms rattling in a jar. Bees were crawling through her skin. She watched helplessly as Grace pulled a hypodermic needle from the bag that the other woman had carried in. Grace nodded to the other woman and said, "Okay" as she removed the taser from her neck, which is where Grace immediately injected her.

Just as Eve was regaining some coordination and movement, the other woman pushed the X26 into Eve's bare midriff—the fire, the M&Ms, the bees and her contorting, vice-gripped muscles returned with a vengeance and then it all quickly faded into a warm, milky black void as she lost consciousness.

Chapter 34

Eve was walking slowly down a long, pitch-black hallway. Too dark to see her hand in front of her face. Her night vision goggles were winking off and on intermittently—a horizontal window frame of ghost-green light illuminated the concrete walls and floors one minute, then plunged into total blackness the next.

Her MP5 was at her cheek pointing wherever her head turned. High-pitched whooshing and pounding filled her ears and seemed to settle in the center of her brain. A giant Taliban fighter, at least eight feet tall, came around the corner, but he moved in slow, liquid motion. Eve pulled the trigger, but instead of bullets, a stream of black ink shot from her barrel and when it hit the fighter he disappeared.

Voices came from somewhere down the hall. Initially, too far away to make out what was being said, but as she continued to walk, they were becoming clearer. Two women talking. A pronounced Irish brogue said, "I think she's comin' 'round."

Eve tried to lift her hand to scratch her very itchy nose but couldn't. As she fought to lift her hand, her heart was pounding almost audibly, sweat beaded on her forehead. Her eyes opened, blinked and squinted at the last of the afternoon sunlight that sliced at sharp angles through a row of high windows at the top of a cracked, aged, 40-foot-tall cinder block wall. The windows were above three large, retractable steel doors, long silenced and rust locked. Although her vision was a bit blurred, she recognized some of the equipment and parts and could tell it was a shipbuilding facility that had been long abandoned. She caught a strong whiff of brackish brine.

Rusting machinery in various stages of disassembly lined the right wall. Giant crusty gears, flywheels, and long, thick steel shafts all akimbo near the end wall. A huge, ship's propeller, missing most of one of its blades, took up nearly half of the space on the left, by the retractable doors. She tried to lift her arm again and noticed it was zip-tied to the wooden chair she was sitting in. But she was able to bend forward and bring her nose to her hand to scratch it, which brought on a bout of intense dizziness and a wave of nausea. She sat back and closed her eyes to fight it.

The two women from the gym were standing a few feet in front of her watching. The one who called herself Grace said, "Welcome back to the land of the living, Love."

The other one said, "How long you remain is up to you." No Irish brogue, but Eve knew a Boston accent when she heard it.

Grace added, "You've been out for a while. My fault. I think I was a bit too heavy handed with the propofol. Your reputation proceeded ya. Needed to be certain you wouldn't fight back. The side effects you're feelin'— the dizziness, nausea, blurred vision, headache and whatnot will all be gone in an hour. Probably sooner."

They were no longer dressed in workout garb. Grace was in skinny jeans, a green v-neck tee-shirt and white sneakers. The other wore tan cargo shorts with a gun grip poking out of one of the big thigh pockets, a black sleeveless tee-shirt and black Nike flip-flops.

Grace stepped over to Eve with a bottle of water, removed the cap and held it to Eve's mouth. She hungrily welcomed the cool, soothing elixir that seemed to fill every arid cell all at once as she took big gulps, nearly draining the bottle. "Easy there, Love. Don't want to vomit it all back up, do ya?"

Eve said, "Nice place you have here. Decorate it yourself?"

The other woman stepped over and backhanded Eve across the face, "We'll be askin' the questions, bitch!" Eve was invigorated by the slap. It cleared some of the fog and she leaned into the pain.

Grace said, "Kelly, no! They'll be time for that."

Eve said, "Anyone ever tell you, Kelly, you hit like a man?"

"Thanks. You'll do well to keep it in mind."

"It wasn't a compliment, dumbass. If I wanted to compliment you, I would have said you hit like a woman."

Kelly went to hit her again and Grace caught her arm. "I said not yet, goddamn it! Where's your self-control, girl?"

Eve said, "Wait. Your Grace and she's Kelly? Really? You don't look anything like her."

"Like who?" Kelly asked.

"Grace Kelly, of course."

"Who the hell's that?"

"Seriously? Rear Window? To Catch a Thief? Dial M for Murder? None of these mean anything to you?"

Grace said, "She later became a princess, right?"

Kelly said, "You mean Meghan Markle."

Eve said, "No. Not… Forget it. I'm sure we're not here to discuss Hollywood actresses who married royalty, so why don't you tell me what you want, ladies."

Grace said, "Why are you here in DC?"

"I'm a consultant for the President's Committee on the Arts and the Humanities."

Grace made a buzzer sound. "Annnnt. Wrong answer."

"Call them and ask, if you don't believe me."

"Oh, I'm sure the CIA set up a nice alibi for ya. But we both know that's a foocking lie."

"Well then why don't *you* tell *me* why I'm here."

"Tell us what you know."

"I know a lot of things. I know that if you travel at the speed of light, you'll reach the moon in just over a second. The sun in eight minutes. But it will take 200,000 years to cross our own galaxy. Pretty amazing, huh? I also know that a cloud can weigh a million tons. The Eiffel Tower gets taller in the summer. I know teeth are the only part of the human body that can't heal themselves. And something you probably already know from personal experience—a cockroach can live a week without a head."

Kelly hit her on the right side of her head with her open hand. Eve saw it coming out of the corner of her eye and turned slightly away, making the blow glance a bit. Kelly's hand caught her right ear, causing the earring's post to poke her neck. Reminding Eve that she was wearing Leo's earrings.

Grace yelled, "Godfuckingdamnit, Kelly! If you can't control yourself, I'll send you the foock outta here! Your last warning. Hear me?"

"John's dead because of this bitch! I want to fuckin' end her."

"You told me you could handle yourself, girl. That this wasn't goin' to be an issue."

"Didn't think it would be. But seein' and hearin' her mouth off's getting' to me."

As Grace and Kelly were face to face, Eve leaned her head forward and clicked her right earring post into the stud, sat back up and said, "You knew Trahison?"

Still facing Kelly, Grace said, "Go outside and cool off. Now!

Or Courtney will deal with ya later."

"Fine!" Kelley said as she turned and headed toward the door at the far end of the building.

As Grace watched her for a moment, Eve bent over again and did the same with her left earring, sat back and said, "And I thought my judgment in men was bad. Holy shit! I sent him to hell. I can help you join him if you like."

Kelly spun around as Grace pushed the stun gun into Eve's chest and yelled, "Shut the foock up!" at Eve and then, "Get the foock outta here and cool off!" to Kelly who watched Eve stiffen and writhe with a big grin, then turned to continue toward the door.

As soon as Grace released the stun gun's trigger and pulled it back, Eve shook her head to clear it and said, "Which is it? Shut up or talk? I'm confused."

It was growing dark and Grace turned on a pair of halogen work lamps on a tube-steel tripod and said, "You're pretty tough, I'll give ya that. I think you may have done this before. Am I right?"

Eve just stared at her, a thin smile, turned her head to spit out some blood from having bitten her cheek. She also noticed they had removed the boot-cast from her left foot. Both ankles were also tethered to the chair legs with zip-ties. Her boot and phone were on the floor next to Grace's cloth bag.

———

Leo was at his kitchen stove frying a burger when his phone pinged. He picked it up and it took him a minute to realize what he was looking at. It was Eve's earring GPS signal. But there was something wrong. It came on for just over a minute and then disappeared. He tried calling Eve again, which he had been doing every couple of hours or so, ever since she failed to show for their Langley meeting that afternoon, but once again, it went directly to voicemail. He texted her with his app again and finished cooking his burger, hoping for a reply this time.

When none came, he was feeling a bit panicky, the apprehension he had been feeling much of the day now amped up greatly, so he rushed to his study and after connecting to the CIA's VPN, he used Overlord to access the Marshal's Service personnel files. Several minutes later Leo dialed Clay Grant's number. He answered on the second ring.

"Hello?"

"Clay, this is Leo. I work with Eve."

"Of course. She told me about you. What's up?"

"Is she with you?"

"No. I've been waiting at the restaurant. I thought she might still be with you. Or perhaps with the President. Was just about to call her. Now you've got me worried."

"She was supposed to come to Langley this afternoon but never showed. I gave Eve a pair of earrings with embedded GPS chips. One of them was activated but then stopped about a minute later. Where's she meeting you?"

"Grazie Nonna. It's on 15th. Three blocks from her place."

"Shit. Something's wrong. The signal came from Baltimore."

"Fuck… Where?"

"South of the city is as close as I can get with such a short signal. On or near the Patapsco River."

"Damn it!"

"I'm gonna text you an address. Meet me here in a half hour with any weapons and tactical gear you've got."

"I'll be there."

"See you then." Leo ended the call.

———

Robin Spinner's phone rang. Right on time. "Hello, Courtney. Saw your text. Got some good news for me?"

"Got her."

"Finally! How?"

"Had a couple women I've worked with before take care of it."

"Figures. That was your initial mistake. You sent men to do a woman's job. What'd they do?"

"I worked up a fake keycard for her apartment building for one of 'em. Found out Eve liked to work out in the gym that's in the building. That's where they got her. Shocked and drugged her. Gym's at the back of the building. They took her out through an emergency exit to their car in the alley. In and out in minutes."

"Where's she now?"

"Baltimore. Abandoned shipyard. On my way there now. What do you want her to tell us?"

"Why she's meeting with the president. You said she's using the name Rose Genest, right?"

"Yup. Used it to rent her place."

"Well, she met with Olson at the White House while I was gone. Used that name. I need to know what they've been discussing these last few months."

"It'll probably take some doin'. She's tough."

"I'm told everyone cracks. Eventually."

"True. But she's CIA *and* Special Forces. They're both trained in this shit, ya know. They go to SERE schools."

"Huh?"

"S. E. R. E. Stands for Survival, Evasion, Resistance and Escape. There are different levels of trainin'. The more valuable your intel, the higher the level. The tougher the trainin'. She's probably done it at least a couple of times. Maybe more. Doesn't matter. My girl's got plenty of experience getting' info from folks typically unwillin' to give it. We'll see how it goes."

"Get what you can."

"And if we come up dry?"

"Either way, she needs to disappear."

"I'm pullin' up to the buildin' now. I'll be in touch."

"Good luck." She ended the call.

As Courtney drove around the building to the water side, out of sight from the road, he called Grace. When she answered he said, "I'm here." Hung up and parked near Grace's SUV, right next to the derelict drydock—the booms of three, long-silenced cranes peered into the enormous, empty, cracked-concrete bay like giant rusty vultures.

The smell of the brackish, salt-laden river filled the windless air. He powered off his burner phone, placed it in the car's cup holder, reached across to the glove box and removed his Glock 45 MOS, which he slipped into his belt at his back as he headed to the door.

"Greetings, ladies," he said as he entered and walked toward them. "Where're we at?"

Grace had a hypodermic needle that she had just filled in her hand. She tapped it with her finger a few times and shot a bit of the clear liquid into the air, removing any air bubbles and said, "Perfect timing. We're just about to get started."

Eve said, "Truth serum? Really? You know there's no such thing, right? They don't work."

"This is my own secret sauce. I start with the KGB's SP-117

formula they developed in the 80s. Add some scopolamine, a touch of midazolam, some sodium thiopental and top it all off with just the right amount of mescaline."

As Grace pushed the needle into her arm, Eve said, "Better be shaken and not stirred."

"We'll see how funny you are in about five minutes."

"Bet I'll be funnier. Ooo, it's already feeling like college around here."

Eve's head began to sway a bit. Her blinking slowed. She chuckled. "Mmm. You should bottle this. Be great on the rocks."

Kelly reached over to slap her, and Courtney caught her arm. "What the fuck're doin'?"

"She killed John. I want a piece of her."

"Look. I know you and young Trahison had a thing back in Boston. MIT's where you met, wasn't it? But I need ya to keep it together until it's time. There are things more important than your vengeance right now. Hear me?"

Eve slurred a bit as she said, "I put four bullets into his fuckin' ugly face."

"You fucking bitch!" Kelly screamed as she lunged at Eve. Courtney slapped her hard and her knees buckled as he yelled, "That's it! Go stand guard outside the door! Get the fuck out! Now!"

Rubbing her cheek where Courtney left a very red, perfectly outlined handprint, a bit shocked and deflated, Kelly headed for the door, her gun in her hand. Courtney calmly added, "When it comes time, I'll let you pull the trigger. Okay?" Kelly turned and said, "Thanks," as she continued walking, rubbing her cheek. To Grace, he asked, "We ready?"

———

Leo and Clay were heading east on the Francis Scott Key Bridge when Eve's earring GPS pinged on again, remained on for just over a minute before disappearing. It had done this three times since they started driving east on the Baltimore Beltway, lasting anywhere from a few seconds to a couple of minutes. Always from the same location.

They didn't know that the signal was being activated whenever Eve was slapped.

Leo switched on the headlights in the descending darkness as he said, "It's coming from directly south of us." He exited the Beltway onto Bethlehem Boulevard, which ran north and south on the eastern shoreline of this section of the Patapsco River, known as Bear and Humphrey Creeks. After a half mile the same street became Shipyard Road.

As they went past the massive Volkswagen and BMW warehouses on their left, they got another ping, This one lasted less than a minute. Leo pushed the gas nearly to the floor to gain as much ground as possible before losing the signal.

Leo said, "She's close," as he slowed down some. They passed the Sparrows Point Shipyard Complex building on the right, lit up with so many floodlights it made this section of the road feel like daytime. The massive building and property bustled with activity as countless trucks with car-carrier trailers were lined up to be loaded with Volkswagens and BMWs.

Clay said, "This building coming up on the right. Looks abandoned." As they got closer, "Faint light coming through a couple of really dirty windows."

"Seems about the right spot. Too much going on everywhere else. I'll drive past it, and we can circle back on foot and take a look.

————

Grace leaned close to Eve's face. Her pupils completely dilated. Grace said, "Yup, we're re— "Before she could finish Eve head butted her right on the nose. The crack was telling as it immediately started gushing blood and she yelled, "Fucking bitch!" and backhanded Eve.

Courtney said, "Shit. Is it broken?"

"Feels like it."

"Got something for it?"

"Ya. First aid kit's in the bag. Bathroom back here in the office," as she picked up the cloth bag and headed to the door that was behind them, her head tilted back, mouth open, hand pinching her nostrils.

To Eve, "You may be more trouble than your worth, darlin.' People want answers, but I just may say fuck it and shoot ya' now."

"By people you mean Spinner, Spinner, chicken dinner, don't you?"

"Ah, so you do know about her. Why've you been meetin' with the president?"

"Cuz, he loves me. He really does. Man, this stuff is good. Do you think I can get the recipe?"

He slapped her face. "Why are you meeting with the president?"

"A simple no would have surfaced. No, that's not right." Her head was wobbling a bit more. "Sufficed. Yeah. Sufficed. That's it. Wait. Where were we? Oh, yeah. The president. Did you know he went to Northwestern? His codename is Wildcat. Shhhh. Don't tell anybody I told you that. Our little secret. Okay? Promise?"

He slapped her again. "Why are you and the president

meetin'?"

"Courtney, you need to learn to use your words. Slap a lot of women in Ireland, did ya? They like it? Most American women don't. And the ones who do? Well, let's just say they're probably not keepers. Most likely renters, if you catch my drift."

Grace came back. She had rolled wads of toilet paper into her nose to stop the bleeding, and the ends were sticking out pretty far. Eve chuckled and started singing, "I am the walrus, koo-koo k'joob, k'koo koo k'joob. I am the eggman, they are the eggman. I am the walrus, koo-koo k'joob, k'koo koo k'joob."

Grace cocked her fist-clenched arm and started to swing when Courtney stopped her and said, "No. Don't. This is pointless. I'm going to end it."

Eve said, "Like you ended the chief justice?"

That got his attention. "What do you know about that?"

"Let's just say I'll never ask *you* to pass the sugar. Uh huh. No way, Jose."

"Go on. Tell me more."

"You make a pretty convincing Bernie Sanders. Definitely should be your Halloween costume this year."

"Starbucks security footage?"

"Yup. Did you know that sugar addiction can be genetic? I mean; I guess there are worse things to pass on to your kids. Lookin' like a walrus, for instance." She started singing again, "I am he as you are he, as you are me and we are all together. See how they run like pigs from a gun, see how they fly. I am the walrus. You are the walrus. She is the walrus."

Grace pulled out her gun and said, "This is foocking pointless. Let's get Kelly back and end this fiasco now."

Eve said, "Like I ended your Hell's Angels. Phhht. Hell's Angels, my ass. More like Heck's Cub Scouts."

Courtney asked, "How *did* you drop 'em?"

"Vincent and Frank? Not the brightest bulbs those two. Brightest bulbs. Get it? They were pretending to be electricians. Oh, come on. That was funny. What? Nothing? Tough audience. Noticed them right away. Like shooting fish in a barrel. No. Angels in a garage. Huh. Makes them fallen angels, doesn't it?"

Courtney stepped on her foot as he asked, "Is that how you got this foot wound?" Eve flinched a bit, but the cocktail coursing through her veins dulled most of the pain.

Something hit the door that Kelly was guarding. "What was that?" Grace asked, then called out, "Hey, Kelly! What's goin' on?"

Courtney said, "Go see, will ya." As she headed toward the door, it flew open and Leo entered, suppressed HK416 at his cheek. Clay was right behind him with his M4A1 carbine. Leo fired twice and Grace dropped. Courtney jumped behind Eve and then dove over a pile of scrap metal as Clay fired, two rounds pinged off the metal. Courtney then bolted through the door to the office that was behind Eve as four more rounds from Clay's gun struck it. Leo ran to the door. His back next to it, gun to his cheek, he spun through and went after him.

As Eve saw Clay coming toward her, his rifle pointing as he scanned the room, it took a moment to register and then she began to sing, "I shot the sheriff. But I did not shoot the deputy, oh, oh, oh."

Leo came back minutes later and said, "He got out a back door and I lost him." Clay was cutting Eve's zip ties from her arms and legs and as soon as they were free, she leaned forward, wrapped her arms around his neck and said, "Hey, handsome. Come here often?"

Chapter 35

Eve awoke and was immediately disoriented, not recognizing the bed she was in or any of her surroundings. She noticed that she was still wearing her workout clothes. She started to get up when Clay came through the door. "Hey there. How you feeling?"

"Like a rug in an elephant disco. How long've I been out?"

Looking at his watch. "Fourteen hours, give or take. How much do you remember?"

"Pretty much all of it, surprisingly. Seems I like to sing when that loopy. I saw Grace go down. Assume Kelly was what we heard hit the door. Did we get Courtney?"

"No. He got away. But without his car. His burner phone was in it."

"Is it here?"

"Yup. Over there on my coffee table."

"I need to shower and get out of these clothes."

"Bathroom's that way. Fresh towels on the vanity. You'll also find some shorts that should fit you and a tee-shirt you can wear 'til we get to your place."

"Wow. You've thought this through."

"Thinking about you and your needs is actually pretty easy."

After her shower, wrapped in a towel, Eve came into the living room where Clay was reading the newspaper and said, "I like your place. Pretty spartan, though."

"Thanks. It could use some colorful touches. Know any artists?"

As she sat on the sofa, "I have a couple of paintings that would be perfect in this room. One there and one over there." As she reached for Courtney's burner and powered it up, "Let's see what we have here. Looks like Spinner's been trying to reach him. A few recent calls and texts." As she typed, "I'm sending Spinner a text message and then it's back off, battery out."

"Let's get you fortified. I make a mean ham and cheese omelet. Up for it?"

"Yes, please. Famished."

As they ate, Eve asked, "What happened after you came for me?"

"I got you into the car and you fell asleep almost instantly. Leo stayed behind. Texted the president to let him know what happened and that you're okay. Then, at the president's urging, he called Alex Marshall, Secretary of Homeland. Marshall contacted the Maryland State Police who took care of the rest. All our names left out. Fed them a hush-hush, national security story. No press. No muss, no fuss."

Grabbing her right earlobe. "Leo picked up the GPS signal from these earrings, correct?"

"Actually, the signal was quite sketchy. Only on for a minute or two several times. It was touch and go. We weren't sure we'd be able to home in on your location. But eventually we got close enough for us to figure it out.

"Leo's pretty sure the proximity to the taser overloaded and shorted them out. We saw those burns on your neck. He's already working on a fix. Something about embedding the GPS chip in an EMP-hardened encasement. He started getting techy and lost me halfway through."

"Where'd they take me?"

"Maryland. An abandoned shipyard at Sparrows Point. Drydock used to be quite active in its heyday. Right on the Patapsco River. About a mile south of the Francis Scott Key Bridge. Shipyard's been inactive since the 80s. While the whole area is experiencing a recent revival, the property contains decades worth of toxic chemicals and heavy metals that, so far, no one wants to tackle."

"How'd we lose Courtney?"

"He ran toward a bunch of active warehouses and businesses just a couple hundred feet to the east, across a rather busy street. Leo didn't want to pursue him too far and potentially raise an alarm from the citizenry."

"Just as well. We'll give Courtney some time to chill. Let him think he's safe and secure. Then I pay him a visit. Probably tonight."

"You up for it?"

"Totally. Your delicious omelet did the trick. So much so, I'd like to show you how grateful I am." She stood from the table and headed toward the bedroom, dropped her towel to the floor at the doorway. "Follow me." She began humming, *I Shot the Sherriff.*

As Clay stood from the table, he said, "The sheriff does shoot back, you know."

"Ooo, I certainly hope so."

———

Robin Spinner was at her desk in her West Wing office when she turned on her burner phone once again, as she'd been doing nearly every hour this morning to check for updates. It had been two days since Courtney told her they had Eve. But she's heard nothing since. And her texts and calls had gone unanswered. So, she immediately perked up when she read the text from Courtney. *It's done. She's gone. I'm out of town for a few weeks. Will call then.*

She opened her top desk drawer and took out her vape pen. Put her feet up on her desk and took a deep draw, blew the cloud into the ceiling and said, "Take that, bitch!"

Chapter 36

It was just before 3:30 a.m. as Eve pulled her car to the curb on Oliver Street, a well-manicured, heavily treed Chevy Chase neighborhood peppered with multi-million-dollar homes. Courtney's was a 3,500-square-foot, two-story, red-brick colonial that sat on the top of a hilly half-acre of well-manicured lawn that sloped down to the sidewalk. The driveway on the left of the house cut into the hill and led to the garage door.

She parked in front of the house that was before Courtney's and sent a one-word text to Leo, *Now*. This prompted him to immediately shut off Courtney's entire security system from his computer.

Leo and Eve spent a couple of hours at Langley. She went there soon after Clay had dropped her off at her apartment. They researched Courtney's house, found photos from the last time it was on the market, some blueprints of the layout in the city hall registry of deeds, and an insurance record of the security system installed by a high-end contractor several years ago.

He had them install the works—night-vision cameras and proximity motion sensors at the front, back, patio, gate, and garage doors, along the driveway, in all the ground-floor windows and across all the yard fencing, every ten feet. It was all monitored and controlled from Courtney's cell phone. Which was how Leo hacked it and shut everything off.

Eve had opted to not wear her boot cast and instead wore a pair of running shoes with the lace on her left foot loosely tied to make room for the bandaging. She quickly picked the lock to the gate on the left side of the house and in a few steps was at the back door, standing by the oval-shaped swimming pool. She had the door open in under two minutes.

She held her silenced Glock in both hands as she made her way, illuminated by her night-vision goggles. She limped somewhat through the kitchen, into the hallway and up the stairs. She paused on the first landing and listened, then proceeded up the next flight to the hallway.

She headed down the hallway and past three open doors, one on the right and two on the left—two empty bedrooms and a book-lined study with a large oak desk—as she made her way to the master bedroom directly in front of her. Its door was partially opened, and she entered. Courtney was on his back, snoring.

She lifted her night vision goggles from her eyes and rested them on her forehead. As she put the barrel of her gun into Courtney's open mouth, she turned on the lamp on the nightstand with her other hand.

Courtney bolted awake, deer-in-headlights look in his eyes. "Let's see your hands," Eve snarled. He sprang them up from under the covers.

She removed the gun from his mouth and backed up two steps. "Get up. Slowly." He tossed the covers aside and stood. She said, "Ah, so it's boxers. I would have figured you a briefs guy."

He was fully awake now. "What the fuck's that mean?"

"Well, since you seemed to really enjoy one of my thongs in my loft, I swore I'd find out what you wore."

"Cameras?"

"Lots." He started looking around. She said, "Nope. Yours are all shut off. One of the advantages of the long arm of the CIA. We can reach all the way into your dreams. Turn them into nightmares." She gestured with her gun toward the door. "Let's go."

"Where?"

She smacked him on the side of the head with her gun, he stumbled, stunned, as she said, "Out. Down the stairs, shithead. And if you think you can get this gun from me, know that you'll be the seventh person to try and you'll be the seventh person to have that be your final thought."

At the top of the stairs, Eve found a light switch and turned it on. As they descended the stairs, he asked, "How did you find me?"

"Did Spinner ever tell you to shut off your burner and remove the battery?"

"She did."

"You should've listened. And speaking of listening, we've recorded every conversation you two have had for the past four months. I'm curious, how the hell did you two meet anyway?"

"When we both lived in Chicago. Before she finished college and got married. We were an item for a couple years. Always ambitious, that one. More than any person I ever met, man or woman. When she got into local politics, I started funding her campaigns. Right from the get-go her eyes were on the White House. Over the years, as she went from councilwoman to mayor to governor then senator, my money grew exponentially. So did her trust."

They went down the hallway and into the kitchen. Eve hit the light switch and said, "Keep going."

He continued, "She knew I wasn't a boy scout and my money

tainted, although she didn't really care to know how. Never asked. But I got things done. All that mattered. As her power grew, so did the things she asked me to do. She also got some things done for me. We're like an old married couple, but instead of being united by love, we're bound by power. Our faithfulness assured by mutually destructive evidence. She brought me into this thing with Trahison, Harrison and your boy-toy Hunter early on. Behind the scenes mostly. In between other gigs I had goin."

"Running guns."

"So, you checked me out, did ya'?"

"When I saw your record, I was surprised you'd never been arrested. Now I know why."

When they got to the back door, Eve said, "Open it." The light from the open door and kitchen window spilled onto the ornately tiled patio and skipped across the pool's surface, creating swirling abstract reflections that danced across the tall wooden fence on the other side. The smell of chlorine wafted in the slight breeze. Then she said, "Go to the edge of the pool, take your boxers off and kneel facing the water. Hands on your head, fingers laced together."

As he did so, she stood behind him, placed the barrel of her gun against the back of his neck, pulled a hypodermic needle from her pocket, removed the plastic cover with her teeth, jabbed it into his right buttock and pushed the plunger. He jolted sideways, "What the fuck was that?"

"A taste of your own medicine." She re-covered the needle and pocketed it as she took a step back. "The coroner will say you had a heart attack and drowned while late-night skinny dipping in your pool. Do you have any last words?"

"Last words? Apart from 'don't kill me,' ya mean?"

"Yes. Apart from those."

"Huh… I've long thought a Roddy Doyle line would make a fittin' epitaph—*Dreaming was only nice while it lasted.*"

She waited a couple more minutes, saw his breathing start to become labored, kicked him in the back, into the water. He flailed and splashed for several seconds before his face contorted as he grabbed his chest, lost consciousness and slipped under. Bubbles broke the surface as he sank to the bottom.

Eve watched for another minute. Then she left the way she came.

Chapter 37

Eve was sitting at the table on her patio with her foot propped up on her other chair. The afternoon sun shuffled in and out of the fast-moving, shape-shifting clouds—intermittent splashes of intense light and filtered shadow moved across the pages of the book in her hands. She took a long tug on the straw of a large, iced coffee she had picked it up at Zeke's on her way back from her therapeutic walk around Lafayette Square Park and set it next to the empty plate that held her recently devoured English muffin.

She had awakened much later than usual, having returned from her visit to Courtney's in the predawn hours and unable to get to sleep for quite some time. When she did arise in the early afternoon, she found herself in an extremely contemplative mood that bordered on agitation and remained uncharacteristically unchanged. She wondered if this was because she hadn't been able to get in her daily run. Running's endorphins tended to even out moods like this. Not today.

And this felt like something deeper. Something even running may not have dispatched. Something that she felt perhaps needed some outside help.

The gusting breeze launched the remaining muffin crumbs from her plate and kept trying to turn the thin, scritta-paper pages of the Bible that Brice had given her a few months ago. She hadn't opened it until a short while ago and read for the first time the inscription he wrote on the title page: *Eve, all of life's answers are found within these pages. C.S. Lewis wrote, "Aim at heaven and you will get earth thrown in. Aim at earth and you get neither." You are in my prayers! Your friend, Brice*

She was replaying some of the things he told her when she stayed with him and his wife in Gloucester after Bonnato's funeral. She found herself drawn to the life of King David—intrigued by Brice's mentioning that he slayed somewhere around 80,000 men in battle. Perked up even more as she discovered he was also an artist—a talented musician and poetic writer. Not to mention a hunky babe to boot.

Up to now, she had considered Michelangelo's statue of David to have derived purely from the artist's imagination, which in many respects was true. But when she had read in the First Book of Samuel that he was described as *glowing with health and had a beautiful countenance and handsome features,* Eve now saw where the starting point of Michelangelo's inspiration had come from.

She had been reading some of the Psalms he wrote. Had just finished Psalm 23 and found herself quite familiar with much of it, since it had become rather culturally clichéd. But Eve was quite taken with verse five. It seemed to leap off the page at her. So, she re-read it a few times… *"You prepare a table before me in the presence of my enemies."* She loved the audacity. The panache. The in-your-faceness of doing such a thing. But it wasn't something that David did, it was something God did for him. God prepared and placed the table.

This wasn't the God she grew up with. The God she knew was as cold, distant, and silent as the statues that filled her church. An austere God who apparently didn't want to hear from her directly and was only approachable through a priest.

But this was a personal God. This was a God whose face David kept seeking. Whose Spirit he kept longing for and begged not to lose.

She was immersed in Psalm 51, noting the headline that said it was the one he wrote right after being with Bathsheba, when he was confronted by the prophet Nathan. Eve, of course, was familiar with the story. Who wasn't? Like most, she'd heard it referenced culturally or in sermons. In one such sermon, she recalled the priest making note that it was spring, when David should have been with his army, but instead he remained in Jerusalem. And so, his first mistake was being where he shouldn't have been in the first place. She had just finished reading the whole story for the first time after finding a footnote at the end of the Psalm that said it was in the Second Book of Samuel.

She empathized with David having the hots for Bathsheba. She knew what that felt like. The all-consuming, mind-altering passion that takes over, voiding rationality and all common sense, justifying its actions with self-indulging blinders on, feeding the flames of fevered lust.

And she was rooting for David when he heard Bathsheba was pregnant with his child and tried to get her husband, Uriah, one of his soldiers, to go home and sleep with his wife. To make the math work. To conceal the soon-to-be-obvious infidelity. It all read like a story torn from the pages of a script from an episode of *Days of Our Lives, The Young and Restless,* or *General Hospital.*

But David wasn't banking on Uriah's honor, his allegiance to his commander and his fellow soldiers who were camped in tents between battles. *"How could I go to my house and eat and drink and make love with my wife,"* Uriah asked. Eve internalized the rest… When my guys are toughening it out. Eating K-rations.

Sleeping in intermittent, unfulfilling fits of twilight dozes on the cold, hard ground. Curled up in quickly dug fox holes. Shivering in the cold night air. Hugging their HK416s.

David even got Uriah drunk and told him to go home, but instead he slept on his mat among David's servants. This was one tough, focused, loyal guy.

Eve knew these traits firsthand. She would have welcomed Uriah onto her special ops team in a heartbeat. That kind of self-denying single-mindedness is a hallmark of a special forces soldier, regardless of branch or country. Uriah was a JTF2 team member, a Green Beret, a Navy SEAL—a member of any one of the special ops groups marked by intense grit and unwavering focus. Since the text called him one of David's "mighty men," she was pretty sure that meant he was also special ops-experienced at putting insurgents into the ground with expeditious precision.

So, when she read how David set Uriah up to be killed, she was upset. Disappointed. Even saddened. By the same token, she was beginning to catch a glimpse of why David was such a popular biblical hero. He was an incredible leader—fearless, intelligent, resilient, creative. But he was also as flawed, fallen, and broken as the rest of us. And after arranging Uriah's death, when he then married Bathsheba, it looked like he was going to get away with murder. But God knew what he did. And sent Nathan the prophet to call him on the carpet for it.

As she continued reading Psalm 51, and seeing what David wrote right after Nathan let him have it between the eyes with both prophetic barrels, she was floored. This was the writing of a man who truly knew God intimately. He owned up to his offenses and was certain he would find forgiveness. Deliverance from guilt. A new heart. Restored joy. She kept re-reading the seventeenth verse—*My sacrifice, O God, is a broken spirit; a broken and contrite heart you, God, will not despise.*

Eve was feeling the assurance David had felt emanating from these lines. Something clicked. This was a parental relationship. An assertion that no matter what you did or didn't do, the relationship between parent and child remained unchanged. An immoveable constant. This was the source of David's confidence of receiving forgiveness.

She was beginning to wonder if this could be the doorway that also leads to the all-too-elusive self-forgiveness, which always feels like grasping smoke.

This was seemingly the root of her mood.

Eve noted that David never felt bad for taking out an enemy. He said that God even trained his hands for battle. He relished having defeated his enemies, completely destroying his foes. And so did his nation. It was his purpose. He was obeying a command. He had clarity.

This too is how Eve viewed her life as a soldier. What every soldier believed. That it was her duty to eliminate the enemy. Her reason for being.

In battle, the decisions to kill the enemy are extremely binary—black or white, on or off, kill or be killed. These are easy choices. Requiring no thought. Just act and react.

But she was finding that in the work she was now doing, well outside of the heat of battle, these choices and decisions were no longer black and white but had become muddled in gray.

Lots of gray.

When the decision of whether a person should die by her own hand or not is no longer binary. When the choice is no longer instinctive, but reflective.

She had made this choice just last night.

And she would be doing it again very soon.

But are these the right choices?

As she recalled the recent conversation with her President, that on his insistence, his command even, that she be free to act on his and the nation's behalf. Her commander in chief trusted her decisions, her instincts, and her judgment.

Eve, in this moment, was coming to grips with her need to embrace the gray.

Accepting that this will be the lens through which she now views her world. That operating in the gray will be inexorable. Her mathematical constant. Her cloud-cloaked North Star.

Something inside her seemed to reset in this moment of acceptance, an almost audible click into place in her heart and mind.

Hopefully, she thought, like David, all that she had done and all that she was about to do would somehow become washed whiter than snow.

Chapter 38

Robin Spinner was on her living room sofa going over her notes for the nationally televised debate that she would be having in two days. She adjusted the arm of her standing reading lamp to better light her pages. A cool September evening breeze came through the partly open window, so she tucked her legs under herself after retrieving her cup of Earl Gray tea from the coffee table.

She and her team had been locked away at Camp David for the last week, rehearsing with mock debates. Senator Gravis, the Majority Whip, was playing the role of her opponent, former president Atout's vice presidential pick, Lance Dattoli, a Senator from Florida who oozed smarmy.

Gravis not only had Dattoli's mannerisms down pat, but the team had armed him with every possible policy and ideological position Dattoli would likely take on the topics that were already set by the network's debate monitors—the economy, the climate, and the Middle East.

Robin was ready. And Dattoli was no stranger. She had faced him numerous times on the Senate floor. She knew she was quicker on her feet and projected greater intelligence and confidence than he did. And she could instantly switch on the genuine charm or the withering heat the moment either were called for.

Dattoli was a bully. And like most bullies, their bluster's much bigger than their bite. Scratch a bully's surface and insecurity tended to be lying just beneath its thin, indignant patina. And she intended to scratch away at it. A lot. She was armed with some comebacks and finely tuned lines and catchphrases that were certain to throw him into bluster-filled responses that should become social media memes and broadcast news sound bites that would likely play until the election, now only eight weeks away.

Atout had yet to agree to a second debate with Olson. And given the nearly one-sided thrashing that Olson rained down on him during their first debate, few were expecting Atout to belly up to the podium for a second helping of humble pie.

So, Spinner's showing will have more riding on it than would ordinarily be the case in a vice-presidential debate. She was relishing the opportunity to flex her position-defining muscle on the national stage. And the smell of blood was in the water—she and her party were buoyed by the latest polls that predict the Olson/Spinner ticket winning by a significant margin.

The President's speech on the first anniversary of the Greater Boston Massacre was still generating buzz. His approval ratings not only went stratospheric after his speech, but they had also only fallen a few percentage points in the three months since. Mostly due to the yet-to-be answered questions of who else may have been involved that still surround the tragedy.

The country wanted closure.

So, the Massacre was still the most significant vulnerability Olson and his administration face. And the president's opponents have turned up the heat to leverage this by increasing outcries for justice every chance they get.

The fact that Spinner helped initiate and orchestrate the cabal, Senator Trahison's bill, and the resulting Massacre had not been lost on her. Which is why her defense of the administration's ongoing efforts to turn over every rock had been so vehement. *So long as no one looks under my rock, that is. With Eve Tuant now out of the picture, I like my odds a whole lot more.*

She was also in a buoyed mood for another reason. She and her husband had just ended a long, pleasant phone call, mostly because of the news Michael had just received and was so excited to share with her.

The ship he commanded, the *USS Michael Monsoor,* one of the Navy's three Zumwalt-class guided missile destroyers, was about to become the global game-changing vessel it was designed to be. The *Monsoor* is one of seven Zumwalt-class missile destroyers to be built by the Navy. His ship, along with the entire class of vessels, had suffered a rather embarrassing history.

The absolute bleeding edge of technology built into these ships—which was initially supposed to be a fleet of 32—made the $7.5 billion price tag for each vessel unsustainable. The entire Zumwalt class had become dismissed as a huge budgetary blunder, and Congress initially reduced the number to be built from thirty-two to twenty-four. And then, adding further insult to further injury, reduced that number yet again to only seven. Captain Spinner's ship was the second of the three built so far.

Until this recent news, her husband found himself on more than one occasion questioning whether he wanted to remain its commander. He once expressed his frustration to her over the fact that he couldn't even fire a single shot from the ship's original weapons system, a 155-millimeter rocket-assisted projectile, because every round cost $1 million. Bad shots were no longer "missed by a mile" but were now "missed by a million."

But even with setbacks like this, and in between his occasional moments of doubt and transfer contemplations, he was still extremely proud of the fact that his ship remained such an incredible technological marvel, featuring the world's most highly advanced stealth capabilities and an all-electric propulsion system.

He was beside himself with excitement at the news that his ship would soon be undergoing a dramatic retooling to host the Navy's first-ever hypersonic weapons to be placed aboard a surface vessel, a transformation that came at a critical point in the newly heated global race for hypersonic supremacy.

While the United States had been developing hypersonic weapons for over two decades, recent advances by Russia and China, made quite public by both countries, had intensified America's urgency to deploy these systems.

Capable of reaching speeds above Mach 5—more than 3,800 mph—hypersonic weapons are nearly impossible to intercept. They achieve this feat by combining their mind-numbing speed with gravity defying maneuverability.

Michael's ship would once again represent a daring leap forward in military innovation. That the stain of embarrassment would soon be completely washed away.

And she was delighted for him.

He also mentioned to her that they would be able to spend more time together during the two years it will take for the ship to be refurbished in San Diego. And she told him that she was looking forward to their being together in January for Olson's swearing in, starting his second term as President of the United States, and hers as Vice President.

She was also experiencing what she could only describe as joy, *so this is what joy feels like,* because she believed Eve Tuant was finally out of the picture. No longer a threat. Gone for good. She felt lighter. Unfettered. Loose. Her sense of humor was back. Something she wasn't fully aware was even missing until Courtney's news had fully sunk in. She read his text several times. *It's done*

She's gone.

At last. Her two-year thorn was finally extracted.

It had been at least four weeks since Courtney's text, but he did say he'd be away for several weeks. She wanted to talk to him. Mostly because she was hungry for the details. And she had questions. Did Tuant reveal anything useful? Did she suffer? *Hopefully.* Where's her body? Will it or should it be found? Can the two women who helped him be trusted? That one she realized answered itself. Courtney would not have used them otherwise. But still, she wanted the assurance.

She also wanted to ask him about the expected delivery of a very special item he had arranged for her. Something that she had paid a very substantial amount of money to acquire. And absolutely essential to her endgame.

Courtney had leveraged his longstanding relationship with his old friend and business partner in the Russian mob, Alexie Nikitinova.

Nikitinova, the recipient of most of Spinner's money, had secured something for which his country had become infamous—its mysterious arsenal of exotic poisons.

Her order was quite special—a recently developed, slow-acting poison that used radiation, but took it to a whole new level. This alpha-particle emitter was completely undetectable and had no known antidote.

Once she administered it to Olson—which, given its tiny size and rapid dissolvability, could easily be done during one of their many meetings—dropped into his coffee, his drink or his food, it would immediately enter his bloodstream, rapidly metastasize to the lymph nodes and pass through the blood-brain barrier. He would experience weeks of gradual physical and mental decline. He'd become progressively more ill until completely incapacitated and inevitably die.

She had no doubt that the fact that he was poisoned would be suspected and discovered.

Iran would then get the blame.

She had already worked out the strategy she would use to make it so. And she would demonstrate her outrage to the world by the retaliatory military action she would order as her country's new commander in chief.

As she gazed into the fire she had started an hour ago, yellow-orange flames pirouetted with abandon behind the arched fire screen, she was thinking of these final stages of her ascendency.

This was her time.

All the planning, the manipulation, the pressure and anxiety, the crafting, the pivoting and power plays, the subterfuge, deception and even death-dealing was all finally coming to fruition.

Sure, she could wait four more years and potentially be the nominee for the next election. The likelihood of her being chosen as her party's next candidate, the heir apparent, was high. Very high. But not guaranteed.

Who knew what the next four years could bring? What unexpected circumstances could come along and ruin the great run she and Olson had worked so hard to attain. The strong economy. Healthy job market. The country's favorable standing at home and abroad.

Perhaps another pandemic could hit, with all the social, economic, and politically destructive fallout that would come with it. Or another war on the other side of the globe that Americans would think in equally polarizing measure that we should do more, and we should do less to either fund it or to end it.

Any number of a myriad of events, circumstances, or conditions could arise at any moment, completely outside of anyone's control.

But it just so happened that whoever was residing in the White House would become the lightning rod for the people's outrage.

Outrage that would become vented in the voting booth.

It never ceased to amaze her how fickle her fellow Americans could be.

And how often the country suffered from collective memory loss. Sure, you've done amazing things for us these last eight years. But that was yesterday. What have you done for me today?

No. There was too much uncertainty in play. Too many potentially blindsiding landmines.

But most importantly, four more years was just too long to wait for what was already set in motion. Hard-won momentum would be lost.

Waiting was off the table.

She would create her own moment to move down the West Wing hallway connecting her office to the Oval.

She was only fifty-five feet and a heartbeat away from the Presidency.

A heartbeat she herself would stop.

So, this is what joy feels like.

Chapter 39

Eve and Clay were at her place, sitting on the sofa watching the news on PBS. They had ordered Chinese food from the Dolan Uyghur Restaurant and Clay picked it up on his way over after finishing his security shift at Supreme Court Justice Amy Thompson's residence.

In front of them, Eve's coffee table held a skyline of open containers of the cold skin noodles and spring rolls they had for appetizers, entrees of Mongolian beef, red chili chicken, and fried eggplant. Clay had put their empty plates into the sink and brought over two cups of coffee he had just brewed to have with the kataifi with pistachio they were currently devouring for dessert.

They watched some highlights from the vice-presidential debate that took place earlier that evening. Eve didn't want to watch the entire debate. Her disdain for Spinner didn't need any more fuel. Highlights and analyses from all the political pundits heartily and unanimously agreed that this was another very lopsided debate in the Olson ticket's favor.

While they said Spinner clearly dominated the debate and controlled the narrative for nearly the entire hour and a half, Dattoli did score a few points over President Olson's mixed record on immigration and the lack of any real headway in the

Greater Boston Massacre investigation. Although it could be argued both of those issues were low hanging fruit. But that was pretty much it.

One of the political commentators, who also had his own show on MSNBC, said that if the debate were a boxing match, Dattoli would be sporting deep, blinding cuts above both eyes that would be swelling shut, a fat, split lip, broken nose, and two cauliflower ears.

The news anchor had now shifted to the Congressional hearings on the Greater Boston Massacre that had been taking place in the House for the last two days.

Many thought the House Oversight and Reform Committee was acting quite prematurely and that these hearings were nothing more than an act of political theatre —smoke and mirrors to divert attention from Atout's sinking ship—an act of desperation deliberately timed to score political points for Olson's opponents just before the election.

Nevertheless, Alex Marshall, Secretary of Homeland Security, was in the hot seat for today's session and Eve wanted to watch her friend deal with Peter Thompson, the Chairman of the Subcommittee, a Representative from the State of Georgia and unabashed Atout sycophant with a penchant for outlandish, polarizing views.

Thompson started the hearing.

"Good morning. The Oversight and Reform Committee and Subcommittee on Domestic Terrorism Intelligence will come to order. The subcommittee is meeting today to hear testimony about the Greater Boston Massacre from Alex Marshall, Secretary of Homeland Security.

"Thank you for appearing before this committee this morning, Mr. Marshall. I would also like to welcome the members of the subcommittee, particularly ranking member Kevin Radcliffe. I now recognize myself for an opening statement and question.

"For years, this committee has worked hard to identify and eliminate weaknesses in U.S. security defenses. Professionals and experts have warned repeatedly about failures to connect the dots and share information between agencies. After-action reviews of various terror attacks have identified individual and systemic failures that remain unaddressed. My first question to you Mr. Marshall is simply this—how did the most horrific loss of American lives since the Civil War happen on your watch? How could such a catastrophic event have taken place without warning? And since logic dictates that destruction of this magnitude would likely require more conspirators than those already identified, what are you doing to find and catch any remaining perpetrators?"

Alex replied, "Thank you, Mr. Chairman. That's actually three questions. And I'll do my best to address each. While it was before your time, Mr. Chairman, you are likely aware that in the weeks and months after the terror attacks of September 11, Congress and the administration worked together to fix the weaknesses which our enemies exploited to carry out their attacks.

"We created the Department of Homeland Security, over which I currently serve as the President's cabinet director. We restructured the intelligence community and launched a war on terror to take the fight to our enemy, all to ensure that a similar attack would not happen again.

"In the years that followed, however, much of the energy behind these reforms has been lost. Budgets were cut and important legislative initiatives were delayed. In spite of that reality, these efforts worked. There has yet to be another significant attack on U.S. soil initiated by a foreign enemy, due largely to the heroes in the ranks of our intelligence community, armed forces, first responders, law enforcement and vigilant citizens.

"But no one could have predicted how our own country would change over the next twenty-plus years. While we diligently prepared for other attacks that could potentially be carried out by adherents to the global jihadist ideology and the rapid evolution and sophistication of terrorist tactics, who in all of our wildest dreams could have predicted that our next enemy, our next momentous attack, would come from within and be self-inflicted?

"Who could have possibly foreseen how our pluralistic but still unified nation would become so polarized, so adversarial, so toxic that the thought of slaughtering fellow citizens seemed a logical solution to gaining political power?

"You mentioned the Civil War, Mr. Chairman. That's the closest time in our 250-year history that parallels our current standing as a nation. Perhaps we have not evolved as much as we would like to believe, as a society, as a people, and as a nation. Every one of us in this room needs to look inward.

"We all have had a hand in creating the soil in which this bitter crop grew and fully bloomed, spreading its seeds of discord, vitriol, and murder. We all let this plant grow wild and undeterred. It was visible to every one of us. And some of us even nurtured it, fertilized it with regular and ample feedings of bile, venom, and cruelty. We are all responsible for this inevitable outcome, including you, Mr. Chairman."

As the camera pointed to the Chairman's reddened face and waited for the outburst that was clearly coming, to his credit he did his best to compose himself as he said, "Let's not make this personal, Mr. Marshall. Please continue to answer the questions put before you by this committee."

"That's precisely what I'm doing, Mr. Chairman. I believe I've answered the first two. To the question of what we are doing to identify any additional members of the cabal responsible for the Greater Boston Massacre and bring them to justice, you must know that I am unable to divulge the details of an ongoing investigation.

"To do so in this room today would only serve to warn and announce our actions to those responsible. But I will say this. You heard the president when he spoke on the first anniversary of this infamous event. There is not a hole deep enough nor a mountain high enough for those responsible to hide that we can't reach and pluck them from by the scruff of their necks.

"I want this committee and every citizen of this nation to know that the brightest, bravest, and most experienced men and women we have ever produced in the counterterrorism community are on the heels of those who remain and are responsible for this Massacre.

"They will be brought to justice with the same velocity and finality that they used to commit this heinous act. You have my word, and you have the word of our president.

"And I want to leave you with this, Mr. Chairman, and esteemed members of this committee. We have an opportunity to carefully improve the security of the United States. This hearing today provides our first step. This step must include bipartisan cooperation. Words do indeed matter.

"We must end the vitriolic rhetoric that has defined this last decade. We need to once again turn our eyes toward the vital issue of safety and security for Americans. For all Americans, despite political party and ideology. Let's stop seeing ourselves as red states or blue states and once again reclaim our heritage as the United States.

"Because if we don't, ladies and gentlemen, then not only did six-hundred and five-thousand, three-hundred and twenty-two of our fellow citizens die in vain, but we should also expect the Greater Boston Massacre to repeat itself.

"And then all of us will be in this room once again, asking these same questions."

"Wow," Eve said. "Not only did Olson pick the right man for the job, I think he may have also selected his successor."

As the news continued to report on other events of the day, Eve began to drift, only partially paying attention. She was mulling over her meeting with President Olson that afternoon at Jackson Place.

The meeting, unlike all the others Eve had with President Olson, did include several Secret Service agents, both from the president's detail as well as the vice president's.

In fact, meeting with the Secret Service was the very reason for calling this meeting.

Both the president and Eve discussed and agreed that the Secret Service needed to be brought into the next part of her plan. That, in fact, it couldn't be completed without them.

To do that, these men and women needed to know and understand what had been going on for the last two years—which meant revealing the actions, identity, roles, status, and the plans of the cabal and its members, both current and deceased.

That afternoon, when the group was gathered, Eve played a few of the most significant wiretapped conversations and read aloud key portions of the transcripts from some other exchanges.

Eve also filled them in on everything that had transpired while she was in Boston, at the lighthouse, and since her arrival in D.C. nearly a year ago. And the president let them know about Leo's encrypted texting app and that it had been installed on his cell.

Jim Benton, head of the President's Secret Service detail, was visibly agitated as he listened. "I wish you had brought me into your confidence about all this sooner, Mr. President."

"I thought about it, Jim, but decided I just couldn't. Too much was unknown and even more at stake. I think you can now see that. It was a tough call, but making tough calls is this job."

Benton got the point and the tone. "Yes, sir. What happens next, Mr. President?"

"Eve has a plan and has already set some things in motion. Eve, wanna fill them in?"

"Yes, Mr. President."

And she did.

Chapter 40

Robin Spinner was in the back seat of her car, returning to the VP residence. She had spent much of the evening schmoozing with prominent donors at a fundraising dinner in the Great Hall at the International Student House, a Washington, D.C. icon, and she was tired. Smiling and glad-handing 120 people for more than three hours will do that.

She had been to the Great Hall several times over the last few years. Every time there she can't help but feel as though she'd stepped back in time and entered a 16th century English manor. The space felt like it could easily have hosted King Henry VIII, with its 20-foot ceilings latticed with opulent dark wood beams, high-paneled mahogany walls, grand yet restrained stained-glass windows, and a one-of-a-kind, majestically ornate, carved-stone fireplace that took up most of one side of the large room.

It's the perfect place to hold fundraisers like this, a truly appropriate setting for a $20,000-per-plate dinner.

During the second event she attended here three years ago, Robin had learned that the Hall was built in 1912 and was designed to resemble Haddon Hall in Derbyshire, England, an 11th-century country house designed like a medieval manor.

She was fascinated by its history and asked for a tour of the house. She became enamored with the opulent library and its intoxicating scent of old-books, and the stunning English countryside garden. She loved the way it all made her feel—resplendent yet intimate.

The highlight of the evening for her was the engaging conversation she had with iconic *Star Trek* actor, George Takei. They talked at length about his passion for social justice and his desire for the Olson administration to continue to lead the charge for policies and laws aimed at defending our nation's immigrant communities, instead of vilifying them, as the last administration had done.

Mr. Takei's position on this issue had clearly been shaped by his having spent part of his youth, from the ages of 5 to 8, in a Japanese American internment camp with his parents.

He was genuinely warm, highly articulate, and charming. And to her credit she had asked him to say, "Oh, my" in his deep, mellifluous voice only once. It all made the time fly by, something that didn't typically happen with these functions.

But in spite of tonight's pleasant experience, Robin was growing weary of events like these, even ones as successful as this one had been, having raised $2.4 million for the Olson/Spinner campaign—although a mere drop in the bucket for the $1.5 billion they were on track to spend by November 4th. She took some comfort in the fact that this was the last one she would have to endure, with the election now only two weeks away.

As her car took a right from Decatur Place onto Massachusetts Avenue and passed by the Embassy of Italy, Robin removed the burner phone from her purse and inserted the battery, which had become her daily routine, checking it at least once. Lately more like three or four times a day. It had been more than ten weeks since she last heard from Courtney. She'd even tried calling him three or four times, but the calls went directly to voicemail that he had yet to return.

So, when she powered it up and saw Courtney's text, she said, "Yes! Finally!" loud enough for Roberta Brown, one of her Secret Service detail who was in the front seat, to say, "What was that, Madame Vice President?"

"Oh, nothing. Sorry. Just talking to myself."

"Yes, Ma'am."

She read: *Call me when you get home. Lots to discuss.*

Five minutes later they drove through the open gate to the Vice-Presidential residence and parked under the porte-cochere. Robin exited the car and went quickly into the house, up the stairs, directly to her study.

She turned on the small desk lamp, removed her coat and dropped it onto the guest chair next to her desk, pulled the burner from her purse and dialed as she sat and leaned back in her desk chair.

She heard a phone ring from the corner of her study and froze as Eve turned on the standing reading lamp next to where she was sitting, Courtney's phone in one hand, her gun in the other. Eve answered and her voice filled the room and then came though the phone in Robin's hand a fraction of a second later. "You look like you've seen a ghost, Robin."

Eve stood, headed over and sat in one of the club chairs in front of Robin's desk as she powered off the phone. Robin was frozen in disbelief. Eyes like saucers. Mouth wide open. "How… what… no way. You're…"

"Dead? No. Your wish didn't come true, I'm afraid. Guess they don't make genies like they used to. Or maybe you just rubbed his lamp the wrong way."

Robin quickly reached into her purse and pulled out a small black fob with a red button that she pushed several times in rapid succession. "We'll see how funny you are when my detail has you on the floor in handcuffs. If they don't shoot you first when they see your gun!" She pushed the button several more times.

Eve spoke quietly. "They're not coming, Robin."

"Bullshit!!" She pushed it several more times. When a few minutes passed, her face drained of color at the realization. Her shoulders slumped and her head dropped forward as she whispered, "Oh, shit."

She was trembling as she opened her desk top drawer, picked up her vape pen and took a long pull, tilted her head back and exhaled a cloud toward the ceiling, then did it again.

Eve said, "I left something on the desk for you." She then slipped her gun into its holster on her right hip under her jacket.

It was a newspaper clipping. An obituary. Robin started reading and said, "What's this? I don't know anyone named Liam Quinn."

"Yes, you do. Only you know him as Courtney Collins. But he's also been Shawn Dempsey and Gerald O'Brien."

She picked it up and read it as she took another big vape draw. The smoke came out with each word, "A heart attack and drowning? Your doing, I assume."

"Yup. Used his own formula on him. As a close friend, one who died because of you and Trahison, once said, 'Don't ya' just love justice when it's poetic?'"

"You'll note the obit's pretty sparse. Mentions his dead wife. Living in Chevy Chase for the past fifteen years. Survived by a son. Rotary Club and Greater Bethesda Chamber of Commerce member. His career as a sales rep for an arms manufacturer. Which is a lie, by the way. Apart from his wife and son, it definitely doesn't paint much of the whole, or for that matter *any* of the real picture. Not by a long shot… You didn't know about his past, did you?"

"I knew enough."

"You knew his money was dirty. But you didn't know how dirty or how he made it. He started quite young. A member of the IRA as a youth in Ireland. He liked explosives back then. Hadn't graduated to poison yet. Blew up some innocent folks. Hightailed it to the States. You two met in Chicago, right? He was running guns for the IRA then. Even more so when he moved to Boston. Then he started to broaden his customer base and moved to DC. Mexican cartels. The Russian mob. Hell's Angels. Despots in Angola, Cameroon, Haiti, and Mali, just to name a few. He was a very busy boy."

"That's bullshit."

"Nope. That's fact. He made some pretty hefty arms deals. One of his biggest was fairly recently. With Iran."

"No way. I would have known."

"Now who's talking bullshit. You didn't even know his real name. And you were never interested in how the golden goose made his money. You only cared about how much of it came your way to support your political ambitions. You didn't give a shit that the goose was himself a murderer—although that *is* something you both have in common. That he was a treasonous opportunist, a career killer who, while he may not have pulled the trigger, he did put advanced weapons into the hands of the dictators, tyrants, and butchers who did pull the triggers and murdered hundreds of thousands of people.

"You only cared that the goose's eggs were golden."

"None of it matters. You can't prove my involvement in anything he did, or anything else for that matter. You have no proof. Zero evidence."

Eve pulled a rolled-up handful of new, blank Earthworks

envelopes and sheets of letterhead stationery from her coat pocket and dropped them onto her desk. "That's where you're wrong. Found these hidden in your file cabinet. We not only know that this is how you let Senator Trahison, Justice Harrison, Hunter Forte and Courtney know when to turn on their burners, we also have recordings from said phones of every one of the conversations you've had with each other and the justice for the past four months. Same for the Trahisons and Hunter from last year. We've got more proof and more hard evidence than we'll need."

Robin was looking pale. Very pale. She inhaled deeply from her vape pen and slowly released the white smoke. "So, what's the play? Arrest me? Just before the election? You may as well kiss Olson's second term goodbye. He'll be tainted by association."

"No. I've got other plans for you."

"What, kill me? How many heart attacks do you think the public will buy before all kinds of suspicions are raised?" Her face was contorting some. She was squinting. Her left hand went to the side of her head, "Congers will welt amslers." Greatly alarmed. "Whass wrong amme?"

"That's the beginning of the stroke you're having."

"Whaa da' fugayu tallin' bout?"

"The neurotoxin you've been inhaling." Eve reached into her coat pocket and pulled out a vape pen. "This one's yours. The one in your hand is what I replaced it with."

Eve placed it on her desk.

The left side of Robin's face was beginning to droop, her left eye almost shut. She tried to lift the hand holding the vape and it only rose a couple of inches, so she slowly opened her grip, and it tumbled to the floor.

Eve stood, went around her desk, picked it up and pocketed it while bending forward, leaning close, meeting Robin's terror-filled eyes and said, "More than 600,000 people are dead because of you. Innocent children, women and men. Whole families. Entire cities. Erased from existence. All by your hand. You had Senator Trahison, his chief of staff, and the Chief Justice assassinated. You were also planning to assassinate our President. My friend. You threatened my family. Had me kidnapped. Tortured. And ordered my death.

"And now you're going to hell, Robin. But hey, look on the bright side, it won't be all bad. At least you'll be among friends. You'll have something in common with several of them—your failed conspiracy, your shattered cabal, and me as the reason you're all there. And how's this for poignant irony—my face will be the last thing you'll see. Good riddance, Robin."

The terror on Robin's face turned to rage and "Fuuuugggggoooooo!" became her last guttural exclamation and her final exhaled breath as nearly every blood vessel in her brain burst at once. Her face contorted in shock for a fraction of a second before going slack. She slumped sideways, lifeless, in her chair.

Eve waited five minutes. Found no pulse. Then left.

Chapter 41

While Eve was still on the first set of stairs leading up from the White House's main floor to the state floor, the cacophonous revelry emanating from the East Room was already substantial, and for good reason. Just yesterday, the country had granted Theodore James Olson his second term as its President by the largest majority vote in the nation's 250-year history. And the people who helped make it happen were celebrating and being celebrated by a grateful president this evening during this invitation-only, black-tie event.

As she reached the top of the stairs and went left down the Common Hall to the tall, open door to the East Room, she was greeted by Steven Penn, the Secret Service agent who always met her at the door at the Presidential Townhouse. "Wowzah!" he said as he saw her, "You belong on the cover of *Vogue* magazine, Eve. Zowie."

And she did.

She was wearing a resplendent, naphthol-red Tadashi Shoji pleated, long-sleeve ruffle crepe gown and white Christian Louboutin red sole, ribbon ankle-wrap stiletto sandals. "Wowzah and zowie are probably the nicest complements I've ever received, Steven, thank you!"

"No, Eve, thank *you*! Please follow me," he said as he led her into the bustling room filled with people engaged in boisterous conversations and laughter, many seated around each of the twenty tables situated throughout. Some were standing by the bar. Others were gathered in groups throughout the large, twenty-two-foot ceilinged room, from which hung three of the most impressive chandeliers Eve had ever seen.

Steven stopped at a table where Leo Burns was sitting with his girlfriend, Audrey, a very cute buxom brunette with a quick smile and intelligent eyes. Eve had met her a couple of times but hadn't had the opportunity to really engage in conversation with her until this evening.

Eve learned that she was a tenured professor of advanced biomedical sciences at Georgetown University and a great match for Leo in every respect. Eve was delighted to discover that one of her closest friends, more like a brother, had seemingly found his soul mate.

Beside Audrey sat Brice Howland and his lovely wife Elise, and next to them behind a chair stood Clay, decked to the nines in a tux that she noted hugged him in all the right places. Steven said, "Here you go, Eve." And to the group he said, "I'll be back later for all of you. The president would like to meet with you privately. Enjoy yourselves!" he said as he turned and went back toward the door.

Clay said, "Wow, you look absolutely stunning," as she headed over to his side of the table. After they kissed, he pulled back her chair and they sat. "Thanks! So do you. I got a wowzah, a zowie, and now a stunning. I could get used to this." Clay, holding her eyes, said, "Get used to it."

Eve introduced the Howlands to everyone and soon the entire table was abuzz in lively conversation and laughter, in between an incredible meal that started out with an appetizer of fruitwoodsmoked quail with quince gastrique and quinoa risotto. That was followed by a lolla rosa, red oak and endive salad with cider vinaigrette and baked Vermont brie with walnut crostini. Then an entrée of thyme-roasted rack of lamb with tomato, fennel and eggplant fondue and chanterelle jus. And for dessert, a pear torte with huckleberry sauce. Each course was served with glasses of wine that perfectly complemented each dish.

While everyone was drinking either their coffees or the Chandon Étoile rosé that was served with the torte, the president entered the room, which erupted in huge applause that quickly became a standing ovation.

President Olson went to the end of the room and stood in front of the wall of huge, arched windows; the lights of DC shimmered their applause in the background. As he thanked everyone multiple times, put his hand to his heart, and finally gestured for everyone to sit, he said, "Thank you all for being here tonight to celebrate this historic moment with me." The room erupted in applause again.

President Olson continued after it abated. "I'm the one who should be applauding you. I simply wouldn't be standing here if not for the efforts of each and every one of you. So, this little gathering is a small token of my deep, heartfelt appreciation for all that you have done to make this possible. And now that we are here, let's not lose sight of why. We were sent here to occupy this house yet again to do more of the hard work we've been doing; to continue the domestic and global progress we've set in motion.

"And this work starts tonight."

Looking around and smiling broadly, "Well, okay, you can start tomorrow." After the laughter, he continued, "We've been given a bellwether-clear mandate from the people of this nation to resume making their lives better and the world safer. We have been and will continue to be able to do this because of each of you. And I'm looking forward to working with all of you over these next four years to mark, not only this administration, but also the future, with a legacy of greater prosperity, deeper peace, and richer hope, not only for Americans, but for our allies and partners across the globe.

"I want to leave you with something Theodore Roosevelt said in 1905. 'Never before have men tried so vast and formidable an experiment as that of administering the affairs of a continent under the forms of a democratic republic. Upon the success of our experiment much depends, not only as it regards our own welfare, but as it regards the welfare of mankind.' End quote.

"I'm looking forward to continuing this successful experiment with each and every one of you. Thanks again and enjoy the fruits of your labor this evening!"

He then headed toward the door, stopping frequently to shake hands and pat shoulders, before finally leaving. Several minutes later, Steven Penn returned to their table and said, "Could all of you come with me, please?" They followed him down the Cross Hall a short distance where Steven opened the door to the Blue Room, an impressive oval room that Presidents typically used to meet and greet guests of all kinds—from kings to kids.

They gaped in awe at the incredibly elegant architectural features of the 30- by 40-foot oval room that George Washington designed. He would stand in the middle as guests formed a circle around him, each an equal distance away. No one was stuck in a corner, which was his designed intent.

From the impressive chandelier to the opulent, gold-gilded Monroe Bellangé-designed chairs and sofa, to the breathtaking view of the South Fountain, the National Mall, and the Jefferson

Memorial through the portico's glass doors and windows, the room overwhelmed the senses.

President Olson entered and gestured to the six chairs arranged in front of the white marble fireplace—two carved caryatids on either side of the mantle, an ornate gilded mirror mounted above it. He said, "Please, all of you have a seat. Thank you for indulging me. I've called you here to thank you. Not so much for myself, but for what each of you did to support a very special woman among you."

Looking and gesturing toward Eve he said, "Eve, words fall short. The entire English language can't do justice to describe the depth of my gratitude for all you've done for this nation, not only through your entire career, but particularly during these last two years. Some of you in this room don't know what I'm talking about and I'm sorry for not being able to illuminate any further just yet.

"Know that the fate of this nation, and my own personal wellbeing, has been held in her extremely capable hands and saved as a result. And because each of you have helped her, supported her, encouraged and prayed for her, you are also very special to me. So, I want to give you each something in return. These aren't gifts so much as earned recompenses."

"First, I've invited the Boston Homeland team to the White House in January, after the inauguration. All of you are also invited to attend. I'll be awarding Captain Evans and Detectives Richard Sweeney and Richard Murphy with the Presidential Public Safety Officer Medal of Valor."

Eve said, "An incredibly fitting honor, Mr. President."

"I only wish I could do more. At that ceremony, I will also be revealing to the nation and the world what they and some of you have done to close the books on the Greater Boston Massacre."

Looking at him, "Leo, I want your encrypted texting app to be used by our entire intelligence and security communities. I've made arrangements with some folks who will help you start a company, organized however you see fit, to contract with you to make it so. The start-up funding is very generous. You are free to continue to work for the Agency, as I'm assuming you will, so this will become a very lucrative side gig for you." Smiling, he added, "Just know I may be hitting you up for a job in four years."

"I don't know what to say, Mr. President. Thank you, sir. Know that I'd do it for free, Mr. President."

"Eve told me you might say that, and while I admire your heart, Leo, I'm also a firm believer that the laborer is worthy of his wages."

Turning to face Clay. "Next, Mr. Grant. I'm told that you've applied to join my Secret Service detail. Your record of service is stellar, Clay. And you certainly would have likely been hired because of it. But Eve's vouching for you made this decision on my part a no-brainer. Welcome to the team."

"Thank you, Mr. President. I serve at the pleasure of the President of the United States."

"You do like saying that don't you, son?"

"I do, sir. I realize how few people actually get to utter those words. It's an honor, Mr. President. Thank you."

"You've earned it, Clay. And it seems you've held up your side of the bargain to serve at the pleasure of Eve Tuant. To me, that's even more important."

Eve said, "Aww, thank you, Mr. President. You're too kind."

"No such thing, Eve. No such thing."

Looking at Brice, he continued, "Mr. Howland. I've heard high praise for your wisdom, counsel, friendship, and your support of this special woman. And she has shown me some of your incredible paintings. I just so happen to be in need of an artist to paint my official portrait. What do you say, would you like the job?"

"I'd be honored, sir. Thank you so very much. I'm… I'm speechless, Mr. President. So, in keeping with recent sentiments, I too serve as the pleasure of the President of the United States of America."

Elise Howland said, "Mr. President, might I make a suggestion?"

"Please do, Elise." Smiling, he added, "But I already gave the gig to your husband."

"Yes, sir, and thank you so much. It will be life-changing for our family. But this is about Eve, Mr. President. If I may be so bold, I know you are now in need of a vice president. And I can't think of anyone who would serve you better than she."

"You have great instincts, Elise. And you're spot on. Which is why I've already asked her to be my next VP. But, alas, she has said no to my offer. And after discussing it with her further, I've come around to agreeing with her decision."

All eyes on Eve. "I too serve at the pleasure of the President of the United States. But I'm able to do so to the absolute best of my abilities and skill sets in other ways."

Looking intently at the President, "I will forever be at your beckon call, sir. You are my President." Smiling broadly, "But more importantly, you are my friend."

With a gentle, loving countenance he said, "And you are mine, Eve. And I count that a great privilege."

Chapter 42

Eve was sitting in an overstuffed leather club chair by a window in the corner of her grandparents' living room with a book on her lap.

She had arrived from Boston nearly a week ago, a day after the group exhibit opening at the Newbury Gallery. Charlene, the gallery's owner, was ebullient and thrilled to be back in her element after so long. And all her artists were clearly buoyed to see each other and reconnect.

The place was absolutely electrified by the national and international news of Brice Howland being selected to paint the President's official portrait. The White House issued the press release only four days prior to the opening and Brice was reeling from the instant notoriety. Had the press known he was at this opening they would have descended on the gallery like locusts. Charlene had agreed with Brice's request not to notify the media of his being at this opening, but they did agree on a date for his next solo show and Charlene was beside herself at the publicity windfall that had just landed in her lap.

At one point during the opening, Brice had taken Eve aside and said, "Listen, I know you want your role in my being assigned the presidential portrait to remain anonymous. And you have my word. My lips are sealed. But I just want to express my deepest, most heartfelt gratitude yet again, Eve."

He got a bit teary, and Eve said, "You've earned it, Brice. Your work speaks for itself. I just showed it to the President. Besides, sometimes good things happen to good people. And you, my friend, are good people."

There was also a palpable sadness in the room, just beneath the surface. It was from the realization they each had as they stood there, enjoying life and art and each other, that more than 600,000 people had had that snatched away in an instant. Since the fire came within two blocks of the gallery, they were acutely aware that they could have just as easily been among them.

Eve wondered if this was a sadness that would never really leave her city. While she assumed that time would likely lift some of its present weight, she embraced the likelihood of a permanent pallor hovering close by from now on—and she thought it to be a reasonable price to pay, considering.

The Christmas tree that her grandfather had cut down from the property's snow-blanketed woods three days ago, and that she and her grandmother had decorated yesterday, was directly across the room by a window, in front of a wall of white, floor-to-ceiling bookshelves brimming with volumes of all sizes, some dating back to the 18th century. Dispersed among the books, a few of the shelves held antique glass bottles and vases, several Huron-made clay jugs and bowls—treasures handed down through centuries of Tuants.

One shelf, near the top on the far right, held a ceramic angel with prominent cracks throughout its body and wings. These were Eve's doing. One Christmas, when she was five, she tried to make the angel fly. Her grandfather did an excellent repair job and even had Eve assist him. His joking with her about it—saying the angel probably hadn't yet completed her flying lessons—as they glued large and small pieces back in place, had made her laugh, greatly assuaged her guilt while deepening her love for this man she called Pepere, but in her heart she called father. Looking at it now triggered these and other fond, formative memories.

A six-foot-wide by eight-foot-tall painting of a young couple pushing a baby carriage in front of the Château Frontenac—an historic, iconic Quebec City hotel built in the late 1800s in the French Renaissance style—took up much of the wall next to her. She had painted it in a realist style—many compared it to Gustave Courbet's work—when she was still in high school and it immediately became one of her grandmother's treasured favorites.

Angels had a ubiquitous presence in this home, an affection that her grandmother had held for as long as Eve could remember. Some came out at Christmas, like the one she broke, and some remained present all year long, like the one that stood on the end table next to her—a three-foot tall, rather chubby white ceramic angel with gray-mottled wings, holding and blowing a long golden trumpet. It reminded her of the artist Fernando Botero's work. As a child she often thought her grandmother must have fed him when no one was looking.

She was reading one of her favorite books, an old, thick college textbook published in the 1940s that was owned by her great grandfather, Emile, titled, *The Literature of England, Volume 1*. It had quite a few of his handwritten notes and sentences underlined in pencil throughout. These gave her glimpses into the man she had never met but had heard so many stories about from her grandfather. Next to a poem that George Herbert wrote in 1633, *The Collar*, her great grandfather had written, "the yoke of God—that he can't get away from" right next to the title.

She was reading a favorite poem that her grandfather had

made a tradition of reading aloud at this time of year, titled, *On the Morning of Christ's Nativity*, written by John Milton in 1629, when Milton was 21 years-old and had just received his B.A. degree from Christ's College.

As a child, much of the poem's language and meaning was beyond her grasp, but as she grew older and then read it more often on her own, as she was doing now, the number of verses that she lingered over grew. Like the ones she was reading now that resumed the angelic theme of the season, the room she was in, and her ruminations—

> *At last surrounds their sight*
> *A globe of circular light,*
> *That with long beams the shamefaced night*
> *arrayed,*
> *The helmeted Cherubim*
> *And sworded Seraphim,*
> *Are seen in glittering ranks with wings*
> *displayed,*
> *Harping in loud and solemn choir,*
> *With unexpressive notes, to Heaven's new-born*
> *Heir.*

The smell of her grandmother's tourtière—ingredients being cooked in the frying pan, the ground pork, onions and spices, and two completed pies baking in the oven—filled the whole house and filled Eve's soul.

This aroma carried within its molecules a lifetime of Christmas memories—sublime moments of wonder, anticipation, tenderness, humor, and joy shared with the people she loved more than life itself.

The back door opened, and her grandfather had an armful of wood for the fireplace. "Can I help you with that, Pepere? Get some more?" Eve asked. He dropped the load into the wood box with a lumbered clatter as he said, "Thanks, but this should do for now. You can get the next load, how's that?"

"Deal."

Her grandfather was adding two of the logs to the three that were well-consumed and radiating on top of the considerably large mound of blushing and breathing coals, when someone knocked on the front door. "Who can that be?" her grandfather asked as he headed over. And then said, "Oh, Mon Dieu !"

Eve slammed her book closed and hopped up from her chair and around the corner to the front door to see two Secret Service agents on either side of President Olson. Her grandfather was shocked into silence for a moment and then said, "Please, come in, sir," as he held the door and stepped aside to let them in. Four agents remained outside, warily scanning the driveway, around the house and surrounding property.

Eve's grandmother came over and stood by her side, mouth agape, removed her apron and fixed her hair as Eve said, "What a lovely surprise, Mr. President! This is my grandfather, Henry. And my grandmother, Geneviève"

As they shook hands, Olson said, "How absolutely lovely to meet you both. And what a charming home you have… *What is* that intoxicating aroma?"

Geneviève said, "My tourtière, Mr. President. French Canadian pork pie. I make them every Christmas and New Year. Would you like some?"

"Oh, thank you, Mrs. Tuant, but I'm afraid I can't stay long. Another time, for certain. I'm sure they taste as heavenly as they smell. Perhaps you can come to Washington next Christmas and make some for us in the White House?"

"I'd be honored, Mr. President."

"It's a date then."

Eve said, "What a delightful surprise to see you, sir! What brings you this way, Mr. President?"

"Two things. First, I'm heading to Ottawa for a two-day meeting with Prime Minster Lafleur. We arranged this a few months ago, after it was determined the next G7 Summit would be held in Alberta this year. We're going to hammer out a topic agenda, determine which economic, security, and other global policies and issues we'd like to cover, and then present an outline to France, Germany, Italy, the UK and Japan for their feedback. I knew you were here and figured I'd stop by to say hello."

"I'm deeply flattered and honored, Mr. President."

"I'm the one who's honored, Eve. As I've already told you, I can't thank you enough for your unwavering dedication and incredible sacrifices. But there's also another reason I'm here."

He nodded to the Secret Service agent on his left, who opened the door and waved someone in. "He was pretty insistent," the President added as Clay Grant entered, wearing his Secret Service "uniform," black suit under his long, black overcoat, removed his sunglasses as Eve was now agape. She quickly gathered herself and said, "Memere, Pepere, this is Clay Grant." They shook hands as Clay said, "I'm honored to meet you both."

Eve's grandmother said, "The one you told us about?"

"Yes."

Clay said, "You told them about me?"

"I did."

He removed his overcoat, placed it on a nearby chair and engulfed Eve in a long hug and quick kiss. They stood side by side—Clay's arm around her shoulder, hers around his waist—

and literally glowed.

The President asked, "Eve, did you tell your grandparents about my job offer?"

"No, sir, I did not."

"I asked your granddaughter to be my next vice president, but she declined."

On their shocked, awed looks, Eve said, "Again, sir, I'm bowled over by your offer. Deeply honored you'd even consider it. But— "

Olson interjected, "Offer still stands."

"Thank you, sir. It's just not the job for me. I'm not a politician, Mr. President. Historically, my opponents end up dead. Not sure putting a bullet into the ranking member of Congress will go over well, Mr. President."

Smiling, "Could be just the thing Congress needs. We'll call it the *brass veto*."

"I'm afraid it might catch on, sir, and then they'll be no lawmakers left."

"Also, not necessarily a bad thing... Kidding aside, I do see your point, Eve, and as much as I hate to admit, as we've already discussed, I agree with you. You're right where you need to be. And I plan on working with you some more in the future."

"I serve at the pleasure of the President of the United States."

"Thank you, Eve. Delighted to have you on my team in any capacity."

Eve added, "Besides, you'll have my beloved right next to you. So, I'll be there by proxy."

Smiling, "I'll take whatever I can get."

Eyes on her, Clay said, "Beloved. A word I've never used before. I like the sound of it."

Eyes locked on his, "Me, too."

President Olson said, "Got one more small gift. Brought an extra Secret Service detail member with me. Clay, I'm giving you two days off to spend here. We'll meet back up with you at the airport."

"Wow. Thank you, sir. I must say, you're the best boss I've ever had, Mr. President, and I've only just started the job!"

"The least I can do for the folks willing to take a bullet for me." At Eve's grandmother's wide eyes, he added, "Not to worry Ma'am. Almost never happens. Getting hit by lightning is more likely." Looking at her with a soft smile, "Your granddaughter's left foot notwithstanding, that is."

The Secret Service agent near the door caught the President's attention and pointed to his watch. Olson said, "Well folks, this has been a short but lovely visit, but I'm afraid we'll need to get going. It was delightful meeting you, Mr. and Mrs. Tuant. I'm sure I don't need to tell you what an amazing granddaughter you have. You both deserve some credit for that."

Geneviève and Henry, nearly in unison, said, "Thank you, Mr. President."

Henry added, "And thank you for the honor of visiting us in our humble home. Oh, my goodness, someone needs to take a picture." Eve handed her cell to one of the agents standing by the door and said, "Would you, please?" They all grouped around the President; the agent took a few shots and handed Eve her phone as she thanked him.

She then went over to President Olson and gave him a big hug, which he returned. "Thank you, Mr. President." Geneviève added her thanks and then asked, "I'm so sorry about the vice president's death, sir. So, who *will* your next vice president be, Mr. President?"

Eyes on Eve, "Gonna be hard for anyone to meet the bar

raised by my first choice." Turns to them, "Still working on it, but I'm leaning toward Alex Marshall."

Eve said, "I had a feeling. Great choice, Mr. President."

"Thanks, Eve. I think so, too."

Eve, Clay and her grandparents stood by the open door as the president waved and then entered the presidential limo, known as *the Beast*, with two agents. The remaining members of his detail entered the other two armored cars, one in front, one behind, turned around in the wide driveway and drove through the open iron gates, turned right and were soon out of sight as they descended the hill.

Eve turned to Clay and said, "Grab your coat. I have someone else I'd like you to meet." After she put on her coat, they went out the back door, through the yard, past one of her grandfather's large, snow-laden metal sculptures, about ten feet tall, a man holding a shovel plunged into the ground.

The falling snow gave the air an earthy, slightly pine bouquet. It crunched like popcorn under their feet as they made their way down a winding path through the trees to a clearing offering a spectacular view of the bluish-white, frozen St. Lawrence River well below the plateaued bluff—the Laurentian Mountains faint in the whitewashed distance.

Eve, holding his hand, led him to a massive oak tree, its snow-shawl covered branches, like bony fingers, poked the tinfoil sky. To the right of the tree's broad trunk stood two granite headstones, side by side, three-feet tall. One with *Henry Tuant* chiseled into its highly polished surface, the other, *Olivia Tuant*.

Eve said, "Mom, Dad, I'd like you to meet Clay. He's someone very special to me. I think you're going to love him as much as I do."

Acknowledgements

I'm forever grateful to my wife, Jennie, whose patience and support of my countless hours in my basement office is what enables me to do this work that I love.

I want to thank Brian Emmet, an amazing friend and deeply insightful editor. I am also very grateful to Wayne Miglore for his eagle eyes.

I'm beholden to William Yeske for *Damn The Valley,* his account of 1st Platoon, Bravo Company, 82nd Airborne's experiences in Afghanistan. And to Edmund Degun and Mark Reardon for *Modern War in an Ancient Land, Volumes I & II.*

As always, I welcome the wonderful support I receive from James Leslie and Phil Halton of Double Dagger Books/Warpath Press.

So, if you end up not liking this book, it's all their fault. Just kidding. It's only Jennie's.

About The Author

After majoring in marketing at Bentley University, Richard spent a career as a copywriter and creative director with advertising agencies serving such clients as Red Lobster, Ducati Motorcycles, Marriott Hotels, and Clorox. He also brought his writing skills to bear for communications agencies that serve nonprofit organizations, including American Red Cross, Wounded Warrior Project, Toys for Tots, CARE, Special Olympics and many others. And he was a frequent editorial contributor to *Fundraising Success* magazine.

In 2000, he helped launch acclaimed author Stephen King's internet publishing debut and the world's first mass- marketed e-book, *Riding the Bullet*. Richard wrote the online ad campaign that prompted more than 400,000 people to purchase and download the novella.

His screenplay, *Graven Image*, placed in the top twenty percent of the Academy of Motion Pictures' Nicholl Fellowships international screenwriting competition in 2014.

Richard is also an accomplished fine art painter. Over the past thirty years, he has exhibited work in numerous solo and group shows. His work was represented by two commercial art galleries in his native Boston and is now represented by a gallery in Chicago, where he currently resides.

Richard and his wife have four adult children and two grandchildren.

Warpath Press is dedicated to publishing the very best in military writing from around the globe.

We believe that writing that is rooted in the human experience of war and conflict, even when written by non-veterans, allows us as a society to examine how human nature responds under extreme pressure. It also gives us a means to ask the big questions about life.

"Military stories" aren't all action-adventure novels. We are committed to finding ways to push the boundaries of "military writing" in new directions, bending it into new shapes that serve society in better ways.

Many of the literary greats of the early to mid-20th century wrote about war and its effects. But Hemingway, Remarque, Dos Passos, Faulkner, Wouk, Greene and Waugh, only had the impact that they did because they were published.

Today, they would likely have been ignored by the major publishers.

And that is why we do what we do.